ONE LAST DANCE

ERNESTO PATINO

ONE LAST DANCE

1

Miami, Florida

"WHAT … WHAT AM I DOING HERE?" Marco Anissi said the moment he opened his eyes.

An attending nurse stood by his bedside. "You were in a car accident. Do you have any memory of it?"

He brought his hand up to his head. "I remember a dog and then … and then I hit something."

"You hit a light pole and you're lucky to be alive. The doctor will be here to check on you later." She adjusted his pillow to make him more comfortable. "By the way, your sister was here an hour ago. She said she'd be back."

Marco lifted his head when Angela finally appeared. "Hi, Sis. Glad you dropped by."

"You sure had us worried, little brother." She walked up to the bed and kissed him on the cheek.

"I know what you're going to say, but I wasn't speeding and it wasn't my fault. If that dog hadn't run in front of me …"

She smiled. "I know all about it. It even came out in the paper. The lady who owned the dog saw the whole thing. She said she felt partly to blame because the dog got away from her when she took him out for a walk. I brought the section so you could read about it." She handed it to him. "Don't be surprised if she shows up unexpectedly. She said she wanted to meet you."

Marco took a moment to read the article. His jaw dropped. "Did you notice the address?"

"What are you talking about?"

"It's the same pole I hit when Susan was killed."

"Are you sure?"

"See for yourself." He moved the paper toward her. "That's not all. Take a look at the date. What are the odds of my hitting the same pole on the same month, exactly ten years later?"

She re-read the article. "It's just a freakish coincidence. Besides, what difference does it make?"

Marco sat up straighter. "I don't believe in coincidences. Maybe … I don't know … maybe someone or something is trying to—"

"Stop right there. I know you were into these weird concepts a long time ago, but …" Angela shook her head. "I really thought you had put them out of your mind after you dropped out of college."

"I did, but this is different. What if … I know you may think I'm crazy. But what if she's trying to send me a message?"

"She? You're not talking about Susan, are you?" She rolled her eyes. "The injury to your head was worse than I thought."

"Okay, so it sounds far-fetched. But listen to me. A few weeks before I dropped out of school, I heard a lecture by this professor from India who had an unusual theory about how an organ like the heart, can possess part of a person's soul. Later, when we met in his office I told him about Susan. I asked if her soul could still be inside her heart that beat in someone else's body. He said yes. Unfortunately, at the time, well, I was too bummed out to follow up on it and I eventually put it out of my mind."

"Look, Marco, why don't you give it a rest? It was an accident—the late hour, the dog. It could have happened to anyone driving on the same road."

"But it didn't. It happened to me." He tapped his chest. "Don't you see? Susan was trying to reach out to me in a way I would understand. If it had happened at a different place, on a different date, I would have missed it entirely."

Angela let out a sigh. "I can see I'm wasting my time. You've decided to make this into some kind of strange phenomenon and there's nothing I can do about it. But promise me something. Don't do anything rash before talking to someone whose opinion you value more than mine."

"I'll think about it." He smiled. "Hey, don't take it so seriously. You're my big sister. Don't I always follow your advice?"

"Yeah, right." She laughed. "I wish I could stay longer, but I've got a chiropractor's appointment in less than twenty minutes. I'll come back to see you first thing in the morning." She gave him a quick hug and hurried out of the room.

2

Two weeks later

AT FIRST, PROFESSOR RANGAN didn't seem to recognize him. "Marco … Marco Anissi," he finally said. "Yes, of course. It's been a long time."

"Ten years." Marco sat across from him. He glanced around the room. Everything looked the same. The picture of Mohandas Gandhi next to a shuttered window, the sagging bookcase, the multi-colored candles atop his cluttered desk. Even the slow-moving ceiling fan that had since developed a wobble. It was as though time never passed.

"What a wonderful surprise. I often thought of you after our last meeting. When I heard you had dropped out of school for no apparent reason, well, it made me wonder. I hope it wasn't because of what we talked about."

"I'm glad you remembered." Marco ran his fingers through his hair. He had a lot to say and didn't want to come across as this crazy, mixed-up person who had nothing better to do than to hang on to old memories and unproven theories.

"The truth is, I was a very confused young man back then. That's why I dropped out of school. I bummed around for a couple of months and then I joined the Army—spent a year in Afghanistan and another in Germany. It seemed like a good way to escape from …" He cleared his throat. "Well, let's just say it turned out to be a good thing for me at the time."

"So, what are you doing now? Did you ever complete your studies?"

"When I got out of the Army, I lost my enthusiasm for it, though I have to admit, coming back here today makes me wish I was a student again. Until recently, I drove a cab. It's not the greatest job in the world but the hours were flexible, and it gave me time to work on my writing, mostly short stories and essays."

Professor Rangan leaned back in his chair and folded his arms. "I always knew you'd come back to see me someday. Though I'm surprised you waited this long. What's this all about, Marco?"

Marco shifted uncomfortably. "I wanted to talk to you about something strange that happened to me. My sister thinks I'm making too much of it and maybe I am. I'll let you be the judge." He took a moment to collect his thoughts.

"A few days ago, I was driving my cab on Old Cutler Road when a dog ran in front of me. I hit the brakes and skidded into a light pole, which knocked me unconscious. I spent a few days in the hospital. Later, when I read about it in the newspaper, I realized the pole I hit was the same pole I struck when Susan—my fiancée—was killed exactly ten years ago." He paused. "I saw it as a sign. Don't you agree?"

Professor Rangan stroked his chin. "Let's just say anything is possible. I'll even go as far as to say the two events could be connected."

Marco stared at him for a moment. "You really think so?"

"Keep in mind we're talking about theories that have yet to be proven. Let me show you something." He got up, stepped over to a file cabinet, and retrieved a thick manila folder filled with old newspaper and magazine articles. "Have a look. You might find it interesting." He handed it to Marco.

Marco glanced through some of the articles. "It's incredible. A man who had eaten meat all his life suddenly loses his taste for it after receiving a heart from a donor who happened to be a vegetarian. Here's another. A young woman who'd lived with a transplanted heart for nearly five years inexplicably commits suicide in the same manner as the person from whom the heart was taken. They didn't even know each other." He put down the article. "It's as if the young woman suffered from the same depression that had driven the donor to suicide."

"Right. There are other stories, though not quite as startling as the ones you just read. If you want, you can take them. Just bring them back or put them in the mail when you're done."

"Thank you. I can't wait to read them all." He closed the folder and set it aside.

"So, what are your plans?" Professor Rangan asked.

"Well, I'd like to follow up on this, maybe work it into a piece—metaphysical things are hot right now. But mostly I want to do it for myself. Get it out of my system once and for all. I only hope the person who got Susan's heart lives in Miami or at least somewhere in Florida."

Professor Rangan nodded. "I must caution you that whoever it turns out to be, may not be receptive, at least in the beginning. So, I would suggest you take it slow and easy. If my theory is correct, Susan's spirit will detect your presence."

"What … if nothing happens?"

"You must think positive, Marco." Professor Rangan waved his finger at him. "Everything depends on it. Without faith, and I'm talking about absolute faith that such things are possible, you will absolutely fail. Trust me on this, and do not for a single moment, doubt you can do it."

Marco rose to his feet. "I took a chance coming here, you know. But I'm glad I did. No matter what happens, I want to thank you for your advice … and for taking me seriously."

Professor Rangan walked him to the door. "I hope everything works out well for you, Marco. And I hope you'll stay in touch."

"I will." Marco smiled. "You can count on it."

•   •   •

"We need to talk, Sis," Marco said from across her kitchen table. "This morning, I met with Professor Rangan from the university. When I told him about Susan, he—"

The stove timer went off. "I have a roast in the oven that needs to cook for at least another five to ten minutes. So, what did he have to say?"

He filled her in on his meeting with Professor Rangan, and when he was through, he said, "I know you don't agree with me, but I've made up my mind. I've got to find out what's going on here. If I don't, I'll probably regret it for the rest of my life."

Angela sighed. "When I said you should talk to someone whose opinion you valued more than mine I didn't think you'd talk to Professor Rangan. I've seen him interviewed on TV a couple of times and he sounds like a total flake. Some of the things he says are so ridiculous I can't understand how the university allows him to teach."

"He's got some strange ideas, that's for sure. And if it'll make you feel better, I don't buy into half of them. But what if he's right, at least about the possibility—"

"Has it occurred to you all of this is happening at a time when you're most vulnerable? It's been three months since you broke up with Samantha and until now, that's all you've talked about."

"You're right. But the fact is, the accident made me see things more clearly. Now I see our break up was probably a blessing in disguise. Sure I loved Samantha, but not the way I loved Susan."

"What about your job? Are you just going to give it up so you can try to find some mystical love that may or may not exist?"

He laughed. "Some job. Driving cranky passengers from one end of town to the other. I guess I didn't tell you—my boss called right after I got out of the hospital. He told me not to bother coming back to work. Their insurance wouldn't cover me unless they were sure I hadn't suffered any permanent brain damage. He said to check in with him in a month or two, but I could tell he really didn't want me." He shrugged. "No big loss.

I've saved a few bucks which should carry me for the next few months and after that, well …"

Angela raised her hands in the air. "I give up, Marco. If going out to look for this person with Susan's heart is what you want to do, then fine. Go ahead and do it. And when you come back all messed up inside, you'll have no one to blame but yourself."

"Relax, Sis," he said, trying to lighten the mood. "Everything will turn out for the best. You'll see."

"Well, it's your life. I just hope you know what you're doing." She got up to check on the roast. "So where will you start? You know it's not going to be easy finding out who got Susan's heart. Doctors and hospitals have very strict policies about releasing that kind of information."

"To tell you the truth, I hadn't really thought about it. But you're right. It won't be easy. Of course, there's always Susan's parents …"

"Is that really such a good idea?"

"No, but they're the only ones who know the person's name. I'll think about it." He stood up. "Boy that sure smells good."

"You want to stay and join us for dinner?"

He smiled. "I thought you'd never ask."

•   •   •

That same day, Marco started a journal—to record his thoughts and feelings as he began his search for the person who had received Susan's heart. If nothing else, it would be good source material for his memoir that he hoped to write someday.

First entry:

This morning, I met with professor Rangan whom I hadn't seen since I dropped out of school. He thought it possible Susan's spirit was still with us, and the accident was her way of reaching out to me. Perhaps Professor Rangan simply told me what I wanted to hear. No matter. I've decided to find the person who received Susan's heart. It won't be easy, and I may even fail. But if I don't do it now, I may not do it at all. My sister is dead set against it, not that I blame her. So, I'll probably not tell her anything until I've found the recipient. Tomorrow I'll call Susan's parents. They may hang up on me, but it's a risk I'm willing to take.

3

F ROM HIS HOME, MARCO DIALED Susan's parents. He got their voicemail and hung up. It was almost a relief that no one answered. He wouldn't have known what to say, not after years of not communicating with them. But like it or not, they were the only ones who could help him, so he tried again two hours later.

"Hello, Mr. Valencia," he said, when the man answered. "This is Marco Anissi. I know it's been a long time and maybe—"

"What do you want, Marco? Why are you calling?" He sounded stiff and unfriendly.

"Who is it?" said a woman's voice in the background.

"I just wanted to see how you all were doing," Marco said. "I hoped that after all these years you'd understand Susan meant as much to me as she did to you." He paused. "Look, I know you still blame me for the accident but as God is my witness I wish it had been me who had died that night."

"There's no point bringing it up again. My daughter is gone. Gone forever. And there's nothing you or anyone can do about it."

"Well, the reason I called was because I need some information." He hesitated. "About the person who got Susan's heart. I know it's a strange request, especially after all these years, but I thought maybe you might—"

"You've got some nerve calling here. I don't know what this is all about, but whatever it is, we want nothing to do with it. I'm very busy and I don't have time to talk to you about unpleasant memories. Don't call here again."

"But Mr. Valencia—"

He had already hung up.

Four days later, Marco received a letter. He pulled out a piece of paper with a woman's name and a Tampa address. Below it were the words, *Good Luck,* which meant the sender was probably Susan's mother, who, unlike her father, had never held her daughter's death against him. He wished he had spoken to her, if only briefly. She would have understood.

Marco knew Tampa well and found the address in a neighborhood where mixed zoning allowed for duplexes, houses and two story apartment complexes. It belonged to a recently painted house with wrought iron bars on the windows and an old, rusting Gran Torino in the driveway.

He drove slowly past the house and pulled over at the end of the street. He couldn't just knock on her door, not without some kind of pretext. He'd pretend to be a freelance writer doing research for a piece on transplant recipients. Maybe throw in a few tidbits from the articles Professor Rangan had loaned him to make it look good.

Marco drove around the block and parked in front of the house. Last minute jitters turned into doubts. Maybe his sister was right—the whole thing was just one big coincidence. He shook his head. He was there, and he had nothing to lose.

Marco walked up to the door and rang the bell.

"Can I help you?" said a middle-aged woman who spoke with a Southern drawl. She wore large curlers on her head and reeked of cologne like the kind worn by little old ladies who stood in line for the early bird specials.

"My name is Marco Anissi. I'm looking for Julia Tinsley. Does she live here?"

The woman shook her head. "We bought the house from her and her husband about five years ago. They were getting a divorce."

"Do you happen to know where she moved to, or if she's still in town?"

She thought about it for a second. "I met her only once, before the closing. As I recall, she planned to move to Tucson, Arizona. She's a dance instructor, you know. I still get mail for her now and then."

Marco smiled to himself. "Thanks, thanks a lot." He couldn't wait to check out Julia's name through the internet.

4

Tucson, ten days later

"WELCOME TO THE Sonoran Ballroom Academy," said a petite, dark-haired woman from across the counter. "I'm Ramona Daniel, one of the managers."

Marco hesitated. "My name is Marco Anissi. I'm looking for a teacher who had been recommended to me." He was distracted by a stream of giggling young girls coming in for a class.

"What's her name?"

"Julia … Julia Tinsley."

Ramona smiled. "She's in the back room. I'll get her for you."

Marco suddenly got nervous. What would she think? A complete stranger wanting to meet her. He turned to leave, just as a woman called his name. "Excuse me. Did you want to see me?" Her voice sounded eerily like Susan's.

He stopped in his tracks.

"I'm Julia Tinsley." She extended her hand. She looked thin, almost too thin, with large brown eyes and high cheekbones that complemented her warm, olive-toned face. Except for the way she wore her long dark hair that came to the top of her shoulders and the tone of her voice, she bore no resemblance to Susan. "The manager said you wanted to see me."

Marco cleared his throat. "Yes, I just moved here from Florida." He tried hard not to stare at her. "I thought maybe you could—"

Her eyes lit up. "What a coincidence. I'm from Tampa. I lived there almost twenty years."

"I'm from South Miami." He smiled. "Like I was saying, I recently moved here and a friend of mine who had met you or seen you dance someplace suggested that I look you up … to take some lessons." He hoped she wouldn't press him by asking too many questions. She didn't.

"Well, I'm glad you're here. But you should know I only take advanced students. Do you have much experience?"

Marco gave a small shrug. "The truth is I've never taken a dance lesson in my life. But I'm a quick learner and I'm prepared to practice every day if necessary."

"We have some very good teachers who can work with you for a few months. They'll teach you all the basic patterns that you need to know. Then if you're still interested, we can discuss whether you want me to be your teacher."

A brief silence. "I'll have to think it over," he said, disappointed. "I really hoped you'd be my teacher, seeing as how my friend had talked so highly of you. But if you can't, well …"

"I'm sorry." She forced a smile. "Why don't you take my card and call me later when you've made up your mind."

"Thanks." He took the card and left the studio.

He had neared his car when he heard Julia's voice. "Marco, wait." He turned around to see her waving at him. "I need to ask you something."

He couldn't imagine what she wanted to tell him. Had she changed her mind? Curious, he walked toward her. He noticed something different about her. Something that he couldn't quite put his finger on.

"I know this may sound crazy, but have we met before? Maybe in Tampa or even in Miami? The reason I ask is because right after you left, I suddenly had this strong sensation that I can't quite describe. Almost as if I knew you from a long time ago."

Marco stared at her for a second. "Well, I suppose it's possible. Maybe we happened to be in the same place at the same time … like a party or a concert." He cleared his throat. "I wasn't going to mention it, but I had the same feeling. I mean about having met before."

She glanced toward the studio. "I have to get back. I have a student waiting for me." She hesitated. "Look, if you're still interested in taking lessons, well, maybe I can make an exception."

He smiled. "Thanks, I really appreciate it." Professor Rangan was right. Susan's spirit had detected his presence. They agreed to start in the morning.

Later, Marco wrote in his journal.

I met Julia for the first time today. Though she was not as I imagined her, I immediately felt a strong connection. Susan's presence was palpable as Julia agreed to be my teacher despite the fact she only takes advanced students. I won't build up my hopes just yet. Though it'll be hard not to, considering that we'll probably spend a lot of time together in the days and weeks to come. Meanwhile, I've got to find some kind of job, something with flexible hours that will allow me to see Julia as often as possible. I don't want to drive a cab again unless I have no other choice. It would be great if I could work in a restaurant. It might even be fun. Tomorrow I'll check out a few places, preferably close to my apartment and the Sonoran Ballroom Academy.

5

"WE'LL START WITH THE RUMBA, which is one of my favorites." Julia wore a beige, loose-fitting blouse and black skirt with a slit on the side that came halfway up to her hip. She led Marco toward the middle of the floor. "The idea is to form a box-like pattern, repeating the words slow, quick, quick, slow until you've completed the box. It's a fairly simple pattern. Ready to begin?"

"Sure." He nodded.

"Okay, then go ahead and start. I'll follow your lead."

He reached to put his arm around her waist and caught a whiff of perfume. "You're wearing Casmir." He said it as though he were making a proclamation.

"I started using it about five or six months ago."

"It smells great." He caught another whiff. It had been Susan's favorite.

They began to dance, repeating the box-pattern several times until Julia stopped and stepped over to a CD player in the corner of the room. "Why don't we try it with some music?" She selected a rumba called *Sabor A Mi* from an old Eydie Gorme album.

"You did very well," Julia said, after the forty-minute lesson. "Next time we'll work on the under arm turn or maybe a cross body lead." She walked over to a table and picked up a spiral note pad. "I'd like to schedule you for at least two, maybe three lessons a week, if it's okay with you. On Tuesdays, Thursdays and Saturdays at 11:00 a.m."

"Great," he said, resisting the urge to chat with her. "See you next Thursday." So far, so good. Everything was working out better than expected.

On the way back to his apartment, Marco stopped at a music store and bought a couple of CDs: one by Gloria Estefan and another by Marc Anthony. He spent part of the day playing them and going over the steps he'd learned from Julia.

"Slow, quick, quick, slow," he repeated. When the phone rang, he could barely hear it over the sound of trumpets and bongos. It stopped ringing.

Later, he played back a message. "It's Angela. I need to speak to you, Marco. It's important. I'll explain everything when you call." She sounded worried.

Marco punched out her number and let it ring six times. No answer. He tried again ten minutes later. She answered on the second ring.

"Hi Sis. I got your message. Everything okay?"

"Look, I don't want you to worry but a doctor from the hospital where you were taken after the accident called this morning and said he needed to speak to you, like right away. Something about the brain scan they did when you were admitted. Here's his name and phone number."

He jotted the doctor's name and number on the back of the business card that Julia had given him. "Thanks Sis, I'll call him right now."

Marco's mind reeled back to the accident. He felt perfectly fine. The doctor probably just wanted to follow up on his progress. He dialed the number.

"Please hold," said the woman who answered. "Dr. Goldstein will be with you shortly."

Seconds later, the doctor came on the line. "The reason I called was because one of my colleagues was going over your scan and he noticed something unusual." He spoke in a calm, deliberate manner. "We'd like for you to come in so we can discuss it and arrange for another scan. Your sister mentioned that you were in Arizona, so I'll leave it up to you how you want to handle it."

"Well, how serious is it? I mean, is it something that I can put off for a few weeks? I'm in the middle of getting settled here in Tucson and didn't plan to be in Florida anytime soon."

"Right now, we don't know what we're dealing with, so the earlier you can do it the better. To be on the safe side I wouldn't wait more than a few days."

A brief pause. "I know it's important and I appreciate that you called, but I'll have to think about it." He thanked the doctor and hung up the phone. Images of Julia flashed through his mind. What would she think if he cancelled his lessons? Would she even care?

By the end of the day, he'd made up his mind. He'd stay for at least a couple of weeks, maybe longer. He called his sister to fill her in on what the doctor had said and about his decision to put off going back to Florida.

"You're making a mistake, Marco. You're letting your obsession with this girl cloud your thinking. The way I see it, she's still going to be there when you return from Florida. If they do another scan and everything turns out all right, you can go back and continue with this crazy plan of yours."

"I feel fine, so quit worrying about me. A few more weeks won't make any difference. If it'll make you feel better, I'll let you make the appointment for me, exactly three weeks from today."

Angela sighed. "All right, Marco. Have it your way. Just promise me that if you start to feel dizzy or have any kind of problems you'll come right home."

"You have my word. If I get the slightest pain, I'll be on the next plane to Miami." He didn't want her to worry but only yesterday he had experienced a throbbing headache that lasted almost an hour. He blamed it on the unbearable summer heat and the fact he hadn't drunk enough fluids.

At the end of the day, Marco wrote in his journal.

Today, I took my first dance lesson with Julia. Did I say dance lesson? I have two left feet, so it will be a miracle if I can last more than a week or two as her student. LOL. Not sure what to make of Dr. Goldstein's recommendation that I go back to Miami for a new scan. I feel pretty good most of the time despite a headache earlier today that went away after I took a short nap. I told my sister to make an appointment for me three weeks from today. By then I should know whether the connection with Julia is real. And if it isn't, well, I'll be more than ready to leave and put the whole thing behind me.

6

MARCO MADE GOOD PROGRESS as he learned one new pattern after another. He especially liked the Latin dances and practiced daily, sometimes two and three hours. On a Saturday, almost three weeks into his lessons, he showed up at the studio a little before eleven.

"Julia called a few minutes ago," Ramona said. "She's running late."

Marco waited almost half an hour before she finally appeared. "I'm sorry," she said, her voice tense. "I rushed to get here as fast as I could."

"I understand." He nodded. "If you'd rather do it another time, it's okay me with me."

She looked as though she'd been crying. "Thanks. I really appreciate it. I'll make it up to you by giving you an extra twenty minutes the next time you come in."

A long pause, followed by a nervous glance toward a group of students coming into the studio.

"I'm a pretty good listener," Marco blurted. "I mean, since we don't have time for a lesson, maybe we can have a cup of tea. Or is it against the rules?" He smiled.

"I'm sorry, I really can't. Perhaps another time. But thanks for the offer."

Marco frowned. "I wasn't going to say anything just yet, but I wanted to tell you that I won't be taking lessons for a while. I need to go back to Florida … to take care of some business." He wondered if she would even care. After all, he was just one of her students.

"I'm glad you told me. When will you be returning?"

"I'm not sure. I'm taking an early morning flight. Anyway, I thought you should know." He waited a moment, then backed away toward the door. "I'll call you in a few days."

"Wait," she said, slowly forming a smile. "Still interested in a cup of tea?"

They strode to a Chinese restaurant three doors from the studio and sat in a booth next to the window. The owner's young daughter took their order for a pot of tea. She left a couple of menus.

"Do you come here often?" Marco asked.

Julia nodded. "Once or twice a week, mostly because it's convenient. I usually order the chicken lo mein or the pork with bean sprouts. Both are very good. You should try them sometime."

"I will." He smiled, grateful to finally be able to talk to her away from the studio.

Julia became suddenly quiet. "I'd like to apologize," she said, haltingly. "It was unprofessional of me to allow my personal life to interfere with my work." She paused to allow the girl to deliver and pour the tea. She continued. "I was late because … I don't know why I'm telling you this. I barely know you."

"I really am a good listener." He smiled. "It's not like we're complete strangers."

She held back a smile. "You're right. As I was saying, my boyfriend and I had a serious argument and I lost track of time. I won't bore you with the details, but I think it's over. Funny how you think you know someone, but you really don't until something happens and then things start to fall apart."

"What … happened, if I may ask?"

"It was nothing, really. You see, I'm a heart transplant recipient and one day I passed out in the bathroom. He went into a panic. I recovered quickly, but after that he insisted I stop working and just stay at home. I refused and from then on, we've had one fight after another." She sighed. "Today was probably our last."

"Well, I don't pretend to know much about relationships, but I'm a firm believer in the old saying 'if it's meant to be, it's meant to be'. And if it isn't, well …" He shrugged. "I'm sorry it didn't work out for you."

She stared at Marco. "I know you may think I'm crazy or something but as you were speaking I had this incredible feeling that you and I had a similar conversation before. Kind of strange. Don't you think?" She reached to take a sip of her tea.

Marco did the same. He was tempted to tell her about Susan but held back. Too soon. He'd just gotten to know her. He'd wait till after he got back from Miami.

"Your trip to Florida … is it business or pleasure?"

"A little of both." He had to come up with something halfway believable. "I need to take care of some financial matters and at the same time remove some gold coins from my safe deposit box, which I intend to close. I'll probably stay a few extra days visiting with my sister, Angela, and her husband."

"By the way, what brought you to Tucson?" She looked at him with a curious expression.

It was a question other people had asked, and he had already come up with a suitable answer. "I'm a struggling writer and I heard that Tucson has a good community of writers. So, I decided to check it out. I'm still not sure whether this is where I want to settle down, but for now I'm enjoying the desert, the mountains, and thanks to you, learning all about ballroom dancing."

They continued to talk until Julia excused herself. "I need to get back to the studio." She stood to leave. "I want you to know I don't do this very often. I mean going out for a cup of tea with one of my students." She smiled. "But I'm glad I did. Call me when you get back and we'll continue the lessons."

His conversation with Julia lingered in his mind, even as he drove back to his apartment. She wasn't anything like Susan, but he liked her and couldn't wait to see her again.

7

Miami

MARCO ARRIVED at the doctor's office a few minutes early. They had been expecting him, it seemed. He filled out a bunch of forms, then followed a nurse to one of the patient rooms. As long as he could remember, he hated having to sit and wait for the doctor to appear. It didn't help that there was no reading material and that the walls were gray and boring to look at, with no pictures except a large medical poster of an exposed brain cut in half. He tried not to look at it, though it was hard not to.

A minute passed and then another. He wished the doctor would show up so he could get it over with. He felt fine. A new scan, a brief meeting with the doctor and he'd be out of there in time for lunch and maybe an afternoon at the beach.

Dr. Goldstein finally appeared. He carried Marco's medical folder and the films from the last brain scan. "I'm glad you were able to make it." He reached to shake his hand. "How do you feel?"

"I feel fine." Marco nodded. "But I'm glad I'm here, so we can get this over with."

"We'll do our best. Let me show you what this is all about and the reason we asked you to come in." He placed the films on the viewer and grabbed a pen from the pocket of his neatly pressed shirt. He pointed to a small white area on one of the films. "It's hard to make it out, but if you look closely it appears like it could be a mass of some kind. We won't know for sure until we get some new scans."

Marco squinted as he stared at the white area on the film. "Was this caused by the accident?"

"No, this is totally unrelated." He glanced through Marco's medical records. "You said you felt fine but have you ever felt dizzy, light headed or maybe even confused for a second or two?"

Marco shook his head. "I do get occasional headaches but they go away after an hour or two. Sometimes I'll take some aspirins."

"Show me where it hurts when you get these headaches."

Marco moved his hand toward the back of his head—the same place where the white area had appeared on the film.

Dr. Goldstein asked him a few more questions and took some notes. Then he paused and said, "Wait here while I arrange for someone to take you to the imaging department for a new scan."

A few minutes later a different nurse escorted Marco to the other side of the building. The scans didn't take long. A young man dressed in gray scrubs took him back to one of the patient rooms. He waited almost twenty minutes before Dr. Goldstein appeared. The look on his face said it all and he braced himself for the worst.

Dr. Goldstein placed the films on the viewer and pointed to the white area, which was larger than before. "It's a tumor," he said, without the slightest emotion. "The good news is that it's operable. The bad news is that it's a risky operation and you may wind up paralyzed. I'm sorry to be so blunt, but I want you to know what we're up against."

Marco took a second to absorb what Dr. Goldstein had said. "Do we have time? I mean, can it be put off a couple of weeks, maybe longer?" He was thinking of Julia. He had just gotten to know her, and he needed time, not a lot but enough to confirm whether Susan's spirit had detected his presence.

"I wouldn't advise it. Those headaches are a warning sign that you can't afford to ignore. I'm surprised you haven't had other symptoms, like convulsions or severe loss of balance. This is serious, Mr. Anissi, so I recommend you talk it over with your family and be ready for surgery within the next few days."

"What about the recovery period? How soon can I get back to my normal routine?"

"Difficult to say. Every patient is different and you may be up and about in a few days. Then again …" He glanced at the viewer. "We'll just have to wait and see."

They continued to talk until Dr. Goldstein's pager went off. "Then it's settled," he said with a cool demeanor. "My nurse will contact you later today and give you all the information you need to know, including the day and time of the surgery."

The reality of what lay ahead sank in as he left the building. He got in his car and just sat there, his mind drifting between what the doctor had said and his conversation with Julia. He regretted not telling her about Susan. He also regretted coming to Miami.

8

"YOU JUST MISSED A CALL from Dr. Goldstein's office," Angela said, the moment Marco walked in the door. "They want you to call them."

"Thanks, Sis." He joined his brother-in-law, Mike, and his sister in the living room and plopped down on the couch. They were full of questions. He filled them in on what Dr. Goldstein had said and about his opinion that the white area on the film was a tumor.

"He wants to remove it as soon as possible. That's probably what the call was about, to let me know when I'm scheduled for surgery." He looked across the room to a beverage cart next to a sliding door window. "I sure could use a drink."

"I'll get it for you." Mike got up and fixed a rum and Coke on the rocks and brought it back to Marco.

"You're going to beat this, Marco," Angela said. "We have to stay positive."

Marco nodded but didn't say anything. After a moment, he put down his drink and got up to call Dr. Goldstein's office. He spoke to the doctor's assistant and scribbled the date and time on a piece of paper. Then he hung up and walked back to the couch.

"They had a last minute cancellation and I'm scheduled for surgery the day after tomorrow," he said, his tone somber. "I have to be there at six in the morning. I don't know if I'm ready for this."

"Mike and I will be with you all the way," Angela said. "Dr. Goldstein is one of the best and I know everything's going to turn out all right. I'll set up the guest room so you can stay with us for as long you need to."

Mike looked at Marco. "What do you say if we take a drive to Key Largo? We can take our time getting back, maybe stop for a drink in Coconut Grove. There's a new English pub that just opened up. It'll help get your mind off things for a while."

Marco thought about it for a moment. "You know what? I think you're right. The drive will do me good." He smiled, though his mind was still on the surgery and the possibility he might not see Julia for a long time. "Maybe we can stop at an oyster bar while we're there. It's been a while since I've had some."

The next morning, Marco got up early and left the house before his sister knew he was gone. He had decided to postpone the surgery, indefinitely.

From the airport, he called her and tried to explain why he'd changed his mind. "What if something went wrong and I wouldn't able to go back to Tucson for weeks, maybe months? Look Sis, I know it's important, but I have to finish what I started."

"Is what you're trying to do with this girl really that important?" she said in a scolding tone. "We're talking about a tumor that could kill you if you don't do something about it, and I mean right away. I spoke with Dr. Goldstein. He said he'd be willing to put you back on his schedule, but only if you call him by the end of the week at the latest. Please, Marco, don't put off doing something you might regret just for the sake of being with someone who may or may not give a damn about you."

A brief silence. "Her name is Julia. I didn't want to tell you about her until I got to know her better. It's hard to explain, but she makes me feel like I did when I started going out with Susan. She's a dance instructor and I take lessons from her three times a week."

"Dance lessons? Now I've heard everything. You're paying for lessons just so you can see her? What if nothing happens? My advice is that you stay in Miami. If you want, I'll call Dr. Goldstein and have him put you back on the schedule."

Marco let out a sigh. Angela made a lot of sense. "Okay, Sis, I get the message," he said, anxious to get off the phone. "I have to go now. I promise that I'll come home as soon as I can. I'll call you often and I won't stay a minute longer than I absolutely have to." He hung up and rushed to the departure gate.

•   •   •

Back in Tucson, he called the studio and asked for Julia. "I'm sorry but she doesn't work here anymore," said the woman who answered.

"What do you mean? Did she take a job at another studio?"

"She collapsed on the floor yesterday while giving a lesson. Paramedics took her to the hospital on north Wilmot."

"Do you know how she's doing? Has anyone gone to see her?"

"Ramona saw her early this morning. She said her condition was guarded and that she won't be able to teach anymore."

Stunned, Marco hung up the phone and headed out the door. He had to at least try to see her if only for a few minutes.

"SHE'S IN ROOM 325," said a silver-haired lady from behind the information desk.

"Thanks." Marco turned and hurried toward the elevators. He got off on the third floor and froze. What if she didn't want to see him? She hardly knew him. He spotted a young, bearded priest leaving her room. "Excuse me, Father." He stepped toward him. "I'm a friend of Julia. I came to see her, but I don't know if she's well enough to have visitors. How is she doing?"

"She's doing okay, I guess, but she's very tired. She's a little scared, so I think she'd welcome a friendly face. I'll keep her in my prayers."

"Thank you, Father." Marco waited a few seconds before entering her room.

Julia lay on the bed with her head propped up on two pillows. She stared out the window at a couple of pigeons that sat on the ledge. Their cooing sounds could be heard through the glass, though just barely.

Marco cleared his throat as he walked up to her. "Hello, Julia."

Julia's eyes lit up. "Marco, what a surprise. I thought you were still in Florida."

"I got in a few hours ago and called the studio to schedule a lesson. That's when I found out you were here. I hope you don't mind … my coming to see you?"

"Of course not." She smiled. "As a matter of fact, I was thinking of you. This may sound weird, but right before I collapsed, I had a strong sensation that I was in Florida. And for a split second your face popped into my head. The next moment I lost consciousness."

Marco smiled to himself. He wanted to tell her about Susan. But he couldn't. It was neither the time nor the place. He'd wait until she was out of the hospital.

"So, how are you feeling?" He moved closer.

"I feel weak and it's hard to breathe, though I'm much better today than yesterday when they brought me in. My heart isn't performing like it should. The doctors think I'll probably need another transplant." She closed her eyes for a second. "They want me to avoid any kind of physical activity, which includes dancing. So, I guess you'll have to find another teacher."

"I don't know what to say. You looked great the last time I saw you. I was really looking forward to resuming my lessons." He paused. "What are they going to do, I mean, besides keep you here for a few days?"

She sighed. "There's not much they can do except monitor my condition. They want me to rest as much as possible and avoid any kind of stress. I've always been very active and the thought of having to stay in my apartment with nothing to do …" She shook her head. "Well, there's no point worrying and dwelling on it. Like the doctor said, I have to learn to think positive."

"He's right. Staying positive is the best medicine." Marco hesitated. "I know we're not close friends, but can I drop by again, to see how you're doing?"

Her lips formed a weak smile. "I'd like that, but I'm supposed to be released tomorrow morning. You can visit me at my apartment, if you like."

He grinned. "I will." His smile faded when a tall, broad-shouldered man walked into the room carrying a bouquet of mixed flowers.

"Just got back from L. A. I came as soon as I heard." The man approached the bed and placed the flowers on a table next to her. He wore a black, tight-fitting T-shirt that accentuated his abs and firm upper body. A large tattoo in the shape of a mermaid covered part of his left upper forearm.

Julia acknowledged him with a smile. "Thanks for coming." She turned to Marco. "This is my friend Max."

Marco reached to shake the man's hand. "I'm Marco Anissi, one of Julia's students," he said awkwardly. "Well, I really should be going. I'll keep you in my prayers." He didn't know what else to say as he turned and walked out of the room.

Back in his apartment, Marco couldn't get Julia out of his mind. He wondered if the guy he had met was her ex-boyfriend. She'd broken up with him, or so she claimed. But that was before her recent health scare. He worried that she might want to get back together with him.

•　　•　　•

Marco answered a call from Ramona. "I just spoke to Julia. She's concerned about your lessons and asked if I could be your teacher, that is if you have no objections."

Though he'd been thinking of taking a break, he said, "Yeah, sure." No matter. It would give him something to do, in between trying to find work and seeing Julia whenever he could. They agreed to start in the morning.

Marco hung around the apartment, took a short nap and then wrote in his journal.

I'm glad I didn't go through with the surgery. It might have been days or weeks before I'd be well enough to see Julia again. However, I didn't expect to find her lying in a hospital bed. Her weakened condition changes everything. I'm not sure how it will affect our budding relationship. The guy who showed up to see her was probably her ex-boyfriend, whom I never expected to meet. Julia is more vulnerable than ever and I hate to dwell on the possibility that she'll want him back in her life. I pray her condition doesn't worsen before I have a chance to tell her about Susan and the reason I came here to meet her. It'll be difficult, but I must stay positive. Can't wait to see her again, maybe tomorrow or the day after.

10

B EFORE THE LESSON, Ramona and Marco took a moment to chat. She had spoken to Julia before leaving the house and confirmed her release from the hospital. "She should be out sometime before noon. Isn't that great?" A wide smile crossed her face.

"How is she getting home?"

"Max, her ex-boyfriend is picking her up. I offered, but she had already made arrangements with him."

Marco frowned. "Do you think they'll get back together? I mean, now that she's sick she'll probably want someone around, to help her do things and take her to the doctor."

Ramona shrugged. "She might rely on him for a few days but my honest opinion is that she wouldn't want to go back to him. Ever heard of the apple pie theory?"

"What are you talking about?"

"Well, my grandmother once told me that a good relationship is like an apple pie. To make one the single most important ingredient is the apple. But you also need flour, butter, and other ingredients. Without them, all you have is a bunch of apples. And the same with a good relationship. The most important ingredient is love. But you also need other things like being able to communicate, having a strong spiritual connection, and most importantly, having the same philosophy of life … how you see the world, the universe … Well, you get the picture. Without them all you have is love, which is great but not enough to bind two people together—like the dough that binds the apple pie."

"So what are you trying to say—that they aren't good for each other?"

Ramona nodded. "Exactly."

Marco held back a smile. "Shall we dance?" He extended his hand.

***

Marco waited a couple of days before driving to Julia's midtown apartment in a complex surrounded by patches of grass and tall trees—unusual for a city with a limited water supply. He had called ahead to make sure she'd welcome a visit.

"Please come in." She allowed him into the living room of her cramped, but tidy apartment. She wore a pale blue sundress and no make-up except for some dark liner around her eyes, which looked tired as though she hadn't slept well. "Can I offer you something to drink?"

"Whatever you have would be fine." He took a seat on the couch and glanced around. An entire wall of photographs of Julia completely dominated the room. Most were from the years she danced competitively, but a few were recent. Like the ones taken at the Sonoran Ballroom Academy during a Christmas showcase. She wore a Santa hat and matching red dress.

"I can see you've had an amazing career," he said, still staring at the pictures.

She carried two cola-filled glasses and handed one to Marco before sitting next to him. "I've been dancing ever since I was a teenager, and yes, it's been a wonderful life."

She let out a sigh. "But now, well, I just don't know what's going to happen. To tell you the truth, I'm a little scared."

"Well, you certainly look and sound better than you did at the hospital."

"I have my good and bad moments. That's when I have to lie down and rest. As long as I don't overexert myself I do okay. I'm supposed to see the doctor tomorrow afternoon, to discuss my options and whether or not I would be a good candidate for another transplant. After I see him I'll have a better idea of what I'm going to do for the next few months." She paused. "I may have to go back to Tampa where I have an aunt and uncle who are willing to take me in, if it comes to that. They're in their eighties, so I wouldn't want to impose on them unless I had no other choice."

Marco nodded. "How are you getting to the doctor's office? I'll be glad to take you. That is, if you haven't made other arrangements."

She thought about it for second. "I was going to ask somebody else, but if you really don't mind. My appointment is at four-thirty at the complex across from the Tucson Medical Center." She took a sip of her drink. "So, how was your lesson with Ramona? When I talked with her she said you were coming in."

"It went well. But I have to admit that it's going to take a while getting used to working with another teacher, even one as good as Ramona." He smiled. "What can I say? I started with the best and now I'm spoiled. Seriously, you taught me so much. I'm glad you changed your mind about taking me as a student. Little did you know I would turn out to be a klutz with absolutely no sense of rhythm."

She laughed. "That's not true. You're an excellent student. In fact I had thought about having you dance in a showcase."

A second later the phone rang and she took her time getting up to answer it. "I can't talk right now." She turned her back to Marco. "I've got company." She nodded. "Let's talk about it later, okay?" More nodding.

Marco stood and walked to the other side of the room. *The Prophet* by Kahlil Gibran lay on the floor next to an easy chair and he reached to pick it up. On the day of the accident, Susan had read to him from one of the sections, the one about love. He swallowed hard as he turned to Julia who was still on the phone.

"Yes, I promise, I'll call you back," she said and hung up. "That was Max, my ex-boyfriend, the man you met at the hospital. He's been very supportive since my heart gave out on me. We're still friends and I know I can count on him for anything." She ambled toward him.

He held up the book. She smiled. "It's one my favorites. An hour ago I sat there, reading from it and dozed off for a moment. Have you read it?"

"Yes." He nodded. "I had never heard of it until … until a friend of mine loaned me her copy and I've been a fan of Kahlil Gibran ever since."

"Funny thing, I had never heard of the book or its author until a couple of years ago when I saw a copy in a used bookstore. It was high up on a shelf. For some unexplainable reason I was drawn to the face on the cover. The sunken eyes staring straight ahead really got to me. I was curious to see what the book was about. I'm only five foot three so I had to stand on my toes to reach for it, and I'm glad I did."

The Prophet was Susan's favorite and he wanted to tell her about it, but he couldn't. Julia faced an uncertain future. Her body had begun to reject Susan's heart. Would it break their spiritual connection? He didn't want to think about it.

They went back to the couch and continued to talk. They had a lot in common: their love of poetry, foreign films, and of course Florida where they were born and raised. When Marco noticed a heaviness in her eyes he knew it was time to leave.

"I've talked your ear off and you probably need to rest." He stood up.

"I am getting a little tired." She walked him to the door and paused. "This is going to sound a little strange, but I suddenly had this feeling again. That I've known you from a long time ago."

There was nothing strange about it, he thought. He could almost feel Susan's presence as she spoke. He flashed a soft smile. "I'll pick you up at a quarter till four."

11

T HEY ARRIVED AT THE DOCTOR'S OFFICE a few minutes early, checked in, and looked for a place to sit. Unlike the day before, Julia's mood was subdued. They sat on a couch in between two large color photographs that hung on the wall, one of the Grand Canyon, the other of a cluster of saguaro cacti on the slopes of a mountain. According to the receptionist, they had been taken by Julia's doctor, whose skills as an amateur photographer were at least equal to his skills as a physician.

Fifteen minutes later, a nurse came out and called Julia's name.

"Good luck," Marco said.

She disappeared behind a door that led to a hallway. After a couple of minutes, he grabbed the nearest magazine and glanced through the pages. An article about organ transplants caught his eye. He read it with interest. No big surprise: patients waiting for transplants far exceeded the number of donors, which meant that only a lucky few would receive one. He stopped reading and tried to put the article out of his mind. But he couldn't. He knew that in time he would have to face the unthinkable. The possibility that Julia might not receive a second transplant.

An hour passed. Julia still hadn't come out. Restless, he got up and walked over to a drinking fountain for a quick sip. A second later Julia emerged from a hallway. She had a calm, almost stoic look on her face as she reached for his arm. "Please take me back to my apartment."

Throughout the short drive, Julia barely spoke, and only hinted that the doctor had been less than optimistic about her prognosis. When they were about a mile from her complex, Marco turned to her and said, "I know you aren't up to going to a restaurant just yet, but what do you say if we pick up a few things and we can cook something for supper? I mean, *I* can cook something." He chuckled. "I'm not the greatest chef but I can cook a lot better than I can dance."

She smiled and thought about it for a second. "I don't think I'm up to it, but thanks for the offer. I just want to go home and rest for a while."

"Look, you have to eat and I have to eat so why don't we do it together? I promise I'll leave right after dinner." He smiled, then added, "Make that after I wash the dishes." She laughed, something she had rarely done since her heart began to give out on her. "Okay, you talked me into it. So, what are you going to cook?"

"I can't tell you. It would spoil the surprise. Seriously, for a time I thought about becoming a professional chef. A few years ago I took some courses at Johnson & Wales in North Miami and later worked at a couple of restaurants."

He dropped her off at the apartment, then drove to the nearest market. He returned thirty minutes later carrying a bag full of groceries and a bottle of wine, a light Chablis to complement the dish he planned to make—his own version of chicken piccata.

Julia had already set the table next to the kitchen. "Let me help you with the groceries."

Marco raised his hand. "No, I'll take care of everything. Why don't you put on a CD that you like and we can listen to it while I cook?"

She selected a recording by Eva Cassidy, who'd become famous only after her premature death from cancer. It began with a tender, haunting version of *Fields of Gold*, followed by *Time is a Healer*, and the ever-popular *Over the Rainbow*. More than once, Julia closed her eyes as she sat and listened to the music while Marco chopped the parsley, minced the garlic, and alternately stirred the lemon-wine sauce, the aroma of which filled the entire apartment. Twice she offered to help but he declined, saying he had everything under control.

Marco worked quickly. He slid the chicken cutlets into a sauce-filled pan and added the final ingredients: unsalted butter, fresh lemon slices, and some capers.

By the time dinner was ready Julia had inserted another CD. A collection of love songs by Andrea Bocelli.

"I'm impressed, I really am." Julia sat at the table. The plate of chicken piccata with asparagus on the side looked like something from the cover of *Gourmet* or *Cuisine*.

Marco lit a candle surrounded by red and yellow rose petals and poured some wine into their glasses. "It's my signature dish. I hope you like it." He raised his glass. "*Bon appétit.*"

She took a bite and savored it for a couple of seconds. "Delicious, absolutely delicious. I haven't had this dish in years and I have to say it's the best I have ever tasted."

"Thank you." He sipped his wine. "I've always enjoyed cooking. It fulfills my need to be creative, like when I write an essay or a short story."

"Have you had anything published?"

"A couple of my essays appeared in a community paper, but that's about it. Of course, like every writer, my dream is to write the great American novel. Maybe I'll get inspired after meeting new people and sampling what Tucson has to offer. I even thought about joining a local writers' group."

They talked while they ate, pausing only to play another CD—a medley of hits from the sixties and seventies. When they were finished, and the wine was all gone, Julia became serious. She finally revealed what the doctor had said.

"It's hard for me to talk about it." She paused. "After I left the office I just wanted to go to bed, hide under the blankets and pretend nothing was wrong. But I couldn't. I had to accept the hand life dealt me." She shook her head. "The truth is the doctor wasn't very encouraging. He said my heart will continue to weaken in the weeks and months to come. He told me to go about my business as long as I don't overdo it."

"What about another transplant?"

She looked away for second. "The doctor said he would put me on a waiting list, but because I had already received one, there's a good chance I might be passed over for a first-time recipient."

"I don't know what to say." He became quiet, then stood up and followed her to the couch. "Look, I know I started out being just another one of your students, but with everything that's happened I think you need someone to help you, to be there for you. That's what friends are for, right?"

She gave a weak smile. "I know you mean well, Marco, but how can I say this without sounding ungrateful. I don't want anyone, including you, to feel sorry for me. I'm a survivor and I've gone through this before. It cost me my marriage and my relationship with Max but that's the way it goes. I believe in fate and destiny and I'm ready to accept whatever happens to me. Like the song says, *No one is promised tomorrow and that is the reason to live for today.* I've taken those words to heart—no pun intended—since the day I had my transplant."

Marco nodded. "Maybe I do feel sorry for you, but not in the way you think. Look, Julia, I just want to help you any way I can. Is that so bad?" He grinned. "By the way, that would include cooking a nice meal for you now and then, or taking you to a nice restaurant, if you're up to it."

"When you put it that way, how I can refuse?" Her lips formed a soft smile. "Before I forget, I want to thank you for taking me to the doctor … and for cooking such a wonderful meal. You really should think about doing it professionally."

"You read my mind. A few days I ago I put in applications at a couple of restaurants. But the competition is fierce, so I don't know when or if they'll get back to me. In the meantime I'll continue with my dance lessons and also do a little writing, maybe about the Tucson lifestyle from a Floridian's perspective. The contrasts are amazing, as you well know."

They continued to talk. When she started to hyperventilate, she closed her eyes for a moment and took a deep breath. "I'm okay now, but I think I should rest."

Marco nodded. "Of course. I didn't mean to overstay my welcome."

She got up and walked him to the door. "Thank you for everything." She hesitated, then reached to kiss him on the cheek.

Later as he got into his car, he touched the spot where she kissed him and he smiled to himself. He was still smiling as he drove away, convinced he'd done the right thing by coming back to Tucson.

That same night he wrote in his journal.

I'm having mixed emotions as I write about Julia. Her visit to the doctor did not go well. She shared part of what the doctor had told her—that she might not be a good candidate for a second transplant. Despite everything, she remains optimistic and I pray that we can continue to get to know each other, albeit under less than ideal conditions. Though unplanned, I spent part of the evening with her. We shared a meal that I prepared and for a moment it was like being on a date. She agreed to allow me to help her in the days and weeks to come, which I took as a sign that she wants me in her life. And when she kissed me on the cheek, I melted inside, knowing she'd begun to see me as more than just another student.

A moment later, Marco added a brief postscript.

What started as a quest to find the girl who had received Susan's heart has turned into a potential life and death drama. I am now faced with a challenge that will test me to my limits. God, if you are listening, please give me the strength I will surely need in the days and weeks to come.

12

"Y OU WERE SUPPOSED TO keep me posted." Angela sounded more like a worried parent than a sister. "So, how are things going?"

Marco took a moment to answer. "Look Sis, you might as well know the truth. Something happened and I can't go back to Miami just yet. Julia collapsed while giving a lesson. It looks like her heart is giving out on her. She won't be able to teach anymore."

"So what are you saying ... that you want to stay there, indefinitely? You have a tumor in your brain, Marco! You have to think of yourself before anyone else and that includes Julia."

"I know what I have is serious, but I feel fine. So, don't worry so much." He paused. "The truth is, ever since Julia fainted, I've gotten to know her better. She's beginning to see me as a friend, not just one of her students. I've visited her twice in her apartment. I even got to cook for her."

Angela sighed. "This is more serious than I imagined. Have you thought about what you're going to do if she dies? You're setting yourself up for something that you may not be able to handle. For your sake and hers don't let this thing go any further. Please, Marco, back off now while you still have a chance."

"I'm afraid it's too late. The connection between us is real and I have to see it through to the end. I may not believe in coincidences but I do believe in miracles. She's on a list for another transplant and if she gets one—which I'm sure she will—she'll be as strong as ever."

A long silence. "You're falling in love with her, aren't you? I wish I could be happy for you. But under the circumstances I'm not, and I wish you had never found her." She finished with a few awkward words, as though convinced nothing she could say would change his mind.

Marco hung up and just stood there, wondering if maybe his sister was right. He was setting himself up for an emotional crisis if, God forbid, Julia's heart gave out on her prematurely. The phone rang.

It was Tracy, the manager of Fronimo's Greek Cafe where he'd left an application. She had an opening for a substitute cook. "We need someone to come in whenever we get busy, or when one of the cooks is unable to work. Are you interested?"

Marco needed the money and quickly said yes. They agreed to meet later at the restaurant for an interview and a quick orientation.

The following day Marco showed up at the studio just before ten. Ramona sat at one of the tables across a dark-haired woman who appeared to be taking notes. A jeans-clad young man with a camera stood next to them.

Ramona waved at Marco and invited him to join them. She made a quick introduction. "They're from the newspaper—Joan Dobson and David Castillo, and they want to do a story about one of our students. I thought of you and the progress you've made in such a short time. Are you interested?"

Marco half-shrugged. "Yeah, sure." He flashed a quick smile and took a seat.

Ms. Dobson began by asking if he was single. Marco said yes, to which she shot back, "By coming to the studio to take lessons, are you hoping to find Miss Right?"

The question caught Marco by surprise. "It was something I had wanted to do ever since I was in college." He tried to keep a straight face. Then he added, "Besides, I was new in town and it gave me a chance to meet people and make new friends."

The interview continued for a few more minutes and ended with a final question. "Do you have any dancing tips you wish to give to all the single men out there?"

Marco thought about it for moment. "My first tip would be: don't tell a woman you know how to dance if you don't. She may call you on it. The second would be, learn at least one Latin dance, such as the merengue, salsa or the rumba. And finally, if you know how to dance and she doesn't, make her feel like she's doing a good job."

Ramona and Marco then got up and stepped onto the floor. They danced a slow foxtrot while the photographer adjusted the lens and took one picture after another. He snapped continuously as the couple danced from one end of the room to the other.

Later, after the reporter and the photographer had left, Ramona and Marco took a moment to talk. "By the way, it was Julia's idea to select you as the subject for the article," Ramona said. "I called her last night and your name immediately came up. She said you were a quick learner, with a natural ability to learn new steps."

"Did she say anything else? I mean … besides what she thought of my dancing abilities?"

"She did mention that you had taken her to the doctor. That was nice of you." She paused. "Did you two know each other from Florida?"

"No." He shook his head. "What made you ask?"

"Well, it was something Julia said right before we hung up. She said it in passing, almost as an afterthought, which made me wonder."

"Said what?"

"That she had dreamed about you. About a time in her life when she was having a hard time getting used to someone else's heart."

Marco didn't say anything. He took it as a sign that Susan's spirit had reached out to him, yet again.

13

THE NEXT DAY, MARCO DIALED JULIA and got her answering machine. He left a short message. She called him back two hours later. "I was out with Max," she said slightly out of breath. "He took me shopping for a new computer. I'm not a high-tech person and he was kind enough to set it up for me."

"I guess this means you're feeling better."

"Actually, I am feeling a little better. As long as I take it easy, I'm able to get around, only a lot slower than I'm used to. So, how did it go with the reporter? I told Ramona you would be the perfect choice."

"Well, it caught me by surprise. But I think it went well. Listen, if you want some company I'm free this afternoon and—"

"I appreciate the offer, but going out the way I did kind of wore me out. I just want to hang around the house, maybe do a little reading. Then I'm going to take a very long nap."

"Well, maybe some other time," he said, disappointed. Afterwards, he thought about her friendship with Max, whom he had assumed was out of the picture. He didn't want to make too much of it, not until he knew for sure that Julia was even interested in getting back together with him. In the meantime, he'd back off a bit, at least for a while.

Moments later, Marco scribbled a quick note in his journal:

I just hung up with Julia who sounded different somehow, almost cold. When she said she'd been out with Max, I didn't know what to think. Maybe they were still friends, and he was merely trying to help her. Maybe she really was too tired to see me. In any case I'll not rest easy until I have a chance to talk to her, hopefully tomorrow or the day after.

•   •   •

Marco waited a couple of days before calling her again. When Max answered he almost hung up. "She's taking a nap. Can I take a message?"

An uncomfortable pause. "I'm Marco Anissi. Just … just tell her I called. Nothing urgent." He hung up and stood there for a couple of seconds. What was he doing there? Were they back together again? Suddenly the phone rang.

"Hello?" He hoped it'd be Julia.

"Hi Marco, it's Ramona. I had a cancellation with one of my students and wondered if you'd like to come in for a lesson at nine. We can work on the Latin dances like the cha cha and the samba. Maybe add some new patterns to make it interesting."

Marco thought about it. He needed something to distract him, if only for the moment. "Yeah, sure. I'll be there."

The lesson went well. Afterwards he and Ramona took a moment to talk.

"Can I ask you something?" Marco said, sounding a little unsure of himself. "I know you and Julia are friends and I wondered if …" He shook his head. "Never mind. I probably shouldn't even be talking to you about it."

She looked at him with a puzzled frown. "What are you trying to say?"

Marco hesitated. "I've become very fond of Julia. But there's a problem. Her ex-boyfriend is suddenly back in the picture. You know her as well as anyone. Do you think she would consider getting back together with him?"

"When you asked me that before I was sure she wouldn't, but now …" She shrugged. "Let's walk outside for a minute. I usually take a smoke break about this time."

She waited until they were well beyond earshot of students entering and leaving the ballroom. "I'm going to tell you something. But you have to promise that you won't repeat this to anyone."

Marco nodded and moved closer.

She pulled out a cigarette from her purse and lit it. "When Julia passed out the other day, she was two months pregnant. She wanted to have the baby, but Max insisted she have an abortion. For good reason. He feared it would put an unnecessary strain on her heart. And he was right. She lost the fetus at the same time her heart started to weaken."

"That explains why he wanted her to quit her job and stay home," he said, recalling his conversation with Julia the day before leaving for Florida. "She said they had argued about it and that's when she decided to break up with him."

"That's right." She took a drag from her cigarette, exhaling slowly. "But now … Well, she's kind of helpless, and Max probably sees it as an opportunity to move back in with her. Julia may feel she has no choice and she may give in to him. He's really not a bad guy, you know. It's just that they don't have much in common. He doesn't even like to dance." She waved at one of her students getting out of his car, then turned back to Marco. "Look, the only reason I've told you all this is because Max is known to have a temper and he may do something stupid if he thinks you're trying to come between him and Julia."

"So, are you saying I should back off?" He shook his head. "Well, I have no intention of doing that. But thanks for the warning."

Ramona's words were still on his mind as he walked to his car. He regretted talking to Max when he answered Julia's phone. He wished he'd hung up on him.

Later he jotted a few thoughts in his journal.

When Ramona told me that Max might try to take advantage of Julia and her vulnerable condition, I immediately feared the worst. He's a known quantity and I can see why she'd want to rely on him more than me. I now realize that I may have made too much of our evening together and she was merely trying to be polite. Maybe she still has feelings for Max. Or maybe—I'll stop there, otherwise I'll obsess about something over which I have no control.

If only I knew what Julia was thinking. If I don't hear from her soon, I can only conclude that she has no interest in me at all. I never thought it would come to this, but like it or not I've got to respect Julia's wishes—good, bad or whatever.

14

Late morning

T RACY FROM THE GREEK RESTAURANT finally called. They needed someone to fill in for one of the cooks, from lunchtime until closing. "I know it's short notice, but we could really use the extra hand."

Marco hesitated for a second. "I'll be there within twenty to thirty minutes." He stepped back and winced when he felt a sharp pain in the back of his head. He gave himself a couple of minutes before heading out the door.

Marco entered the kitchen and took a deep whiff. The unmistakable aroma of lamb cooking in the oven filled the air. "Hmm … smells good," he said to Tracy. "I think I'm going to enjoy working here. Where do I start?"

Tracy introduced him to the head chef, a jovial, gray-haired man who gave him an apron and went over the menu. "You can start by making the salad, enough for about thirty servings," he said with a heavy Greek accent. He retrieved a thick spiral notebook filled with handwritten recipes and opened it to the page marked salads. "Just follow the recipe. Later you can help me with the chicken skewers. And if we have time we'll bake some baklava for tomorrow." The familiar theme song from Zorba the Greek played in the background and the chef put his arms above his head. He began to dance, to the amusement of Tracy, Marco and one of the servers who shouted, "Opa!"

The day went quickly. When Marco's phone rang just before 3:00 p.m. he hesitated before answering it.

"Dr. Goldstein would like to speak to you," said a woman with a hint of a Spanish accent. "Hold on while I put him through."

Marco stood motionless for a couple of seconds. Should he explain to Dr. Goldstein why he couldn't schedule the surgery just yet? Would he understand? Probably not. "I'm at work and I can't talk to him right now. Tell him I'll call him first thing in the morning." He pressed the Off key.

•　　　•　　　•

The next day, Marco picked up Dr. Goldstein's card and dialed the number. When a woman answered and put him on hold, he hung up. He'd try again later. Meanwhile, he had twenty minutes to practice his steps before heading over to the studio for his ten o'clock lesson.

Ramona greeted him with a hug and started by going over the steps from the previous lesson. At the opposite end of the room, a young man and his raven-haired partner took to the floor. A slow rumba played in the background. Their bodies pressed tightly against each other, they danced as though they were lovers.

Marco smiled and said with a tinge of envy in his voice, "Are they boyfriend and girlfriend?"

Ramona let out a chuckle. "No, they're just dance partners practicing for a competition. She's married with a two-year-old daughter and he's got a steady girlfriend. They're good dancers and they want everyone to believe they're a hot couple, so they will stand out from the rest of the crowd. That's what it's all about."

After his lesson, Marco left the studio. He had neared his car when a man's voice called from behind and he turned around slowly. It was Max, Julia's ex-boyfriend.

Max took a step toward him. "I know all about you, but you're wasting your time," he said with a smirk on his face.

"What are you talking about?" Marco carried a pair of dancing shoes and set them down on the roof of his car.

"Julia said that you took her to the doctor the other day and that you had dinner together. She said you were one of her better students." He crossed his arms and stared at him for moment. "Look, I think I know what's going on here. You like her, and with everything that's happened, you want to be there for her as a friend. Am I right?"

Marco nodded.

"Well, I hate to burst your bubble, but Julia isn't interested in you, not even as a friend. But she's too polite to tell you she doesn't want you calling her." He relaxed his arms and looked around as though to make sure no one listened. "The fact is, she and I are getting back together. So, if you really care about her as a friend or whatever, you'll leave her alone. I think I know her better than anyone, and the only person she really needs right now is me." He slapped his chest with the palm of his hand.

"You may be right, but I'd like to hear it directly from Julia. Whether you like it or not she and I—"

"Didn't you hear me?" Max said, a hostile edge to his voice. "She wants you to leave her alone. You seem like a reasonable guy, so just back off and stay out of her life."

And if I don't? Marco wanted to say, but he didn't. The guy was a hothead—no point discussing it with him. After an uncomfortable silence, he finally said, "I get the message," and got in his car. When he pulled out of the lot, he glanced in his rearview mirror and saw Max standing in the same spot with his hands on his hips and a scowl on his face. He had a feeling he'd not heard the last from him.

Back in his apartment, Marco thought about Max. Was he telling the truth? Only one way to find out. He picked up the phone and dialed Julia's number. When her voice mail answered, he hung up. He poured himself a glass of wine and waited a half hour before dialing again. No response. He hesitated for a second, then left a message.

"Julia, I really need to speak to you. Can you please call me, no matter how late it is?" He hung up and sipped his wine. He stayed home the rest of the day, hoping to hear from her. When he finally went to bed, he couldn't stop thinking of Julia. Maybe Max was right—she wanted nothing to do with him. He had a fitful night's sleep as he drifted in and out of a strange dream that alternated between memories of Susan and a strong sensation that Julia's death was imminent.

15

Mid-morning

WHEN THE PHONE RANG, Marco rushed to answer it. He hoped it'd be Julia.

"Hi, Marco. It's Tracy. The assistant cook is still sick and I wondered if you could fill in for him again."

Disappointed, he let out a sigh. "I don't know … I'm expecting an important phone call and I may be busy for the rest of the day. I wish I could help you but—"

"It wouldn't have to be for the whole day. Could you at least help us out for the lunch crowd?" She sounded desperate.

Marco hesitated. "Okay. I'll be there as soon as I can." Even as he hung up, all he could think of was Julia, and he wondered why she hadn't returned his call. Should he try her again? He shook his head. He'd wait till the end of day or maybe even tomorrow.

Tracy thanked Marco the moment he entered the restaurant. "We're expecting a big lunch crowd. The theater across the street is having a film festival—movies from the forties and fifties."

Through the window facing the street, Marco read the titles on the marquee: *Citizen Kane, Some Like It Hot, On the Waterfront, The Maltese Falcon.*

By 3:30 p.m., the restaurant was mostly empty. Marco finally took a quick break on the patio. His mind soon drifted to thoughts of Julia and the possibility that she and Max were back together again. When his phone rang, he recognized Julia's number. He took a deep breath before answering it.

"I'm sorry I didn't get back to you right way." She hesitated. "You've been a good friend and I don't know how to say this, without sounding ungrateful. I … think it would be best if you not call me anymore. I know what you're thinking and I wish I didn't have to do this, but—"

"Is this about you and Max?"

"Yes," she said, after a pause. "We miss each other and we're willing to give our relationship another try. He's been very supportive during the past few days. In a way I think this crisis has brought us closer to one another. He's really a wonderful person … very caring, and always willing to give me my space whenever I need it."

"Are you in love with him?"

A long silence. "It's complicated. I guess the best answer I can give you is I think I am. Please try to understand that I'm in a difficult position with an uncertain future and very few options. You're a great guy, Marco. Under different circumstances, we might have … well, you know what I'm trying to say."

"I understand," he said softly. He wanted to tell her she was making a mistake, but he didn't. He wished her luck and quietly hung up.

He stood there for several seconds, his brain trying to absorb what Julia had said. Whatever dreams he had of being with her had suddenly vanished. After a moment, he went back to work and decided to stay until closing. He needed to focus on something other than Julia, at least for the rest of the day.

He got home around 10:15 p.m., poured himself a glass of wine and sat at the kitchen table. His mind still on Julia, he wrote her a letter.

Dear Julia,

This is very difficult for me to write because I had wanted to say these things in person. But as I got to know you better, I just kept putting it off, thinking I would tell you later. Maybe if I had opened up to you sooner, things would have turned out differently. We'll never know.

I guess I should start at the beginning. Ten years ago, my fiancée, Susan, was killed in a car accident. I was driving when the car slid out of control and struck a light pole. That same night, her parents made the unselfish decision to donate her heart. As you may have guessed, you were the recipient. For years I lived with the pain and guilt of the tragedy that can never be erased from my mind.

Everything changed a few months ago when I happened to be driving at night on the same road. A dog crossed my path, and the car slid out of control, slamming into a light pole. The same pole I struck while riding with Susan, exactly ten years ago.

Coincidence? Not if you believe in spiritual connections. I saw it as a sign that Susan had reached out to me. From that moment I knew I had to meet the girl with Susan's heart.

So now you know why I came here to meet you. Please don't feel that you have to answer this letter or even call me. I'll be okay. I'm a survivor, just like you.

Forever, Marco

He took a sip of wine and read what he had written, then placed the letter in an envelope. He'd mail it in the morning.

A half hour later, he fell asleep on the couch. He awoke around 3:00 a.m. His heart pounded as he tried to shake the images of a dream that took him back to the night Susan was killed. But it was Julia's face he saw sitting next to him in the crumpled car, and it frightened him. So much so, that he couldn't go back to sleep for the rest of the night.

16

THE NEXT MORNING, Marco answered a knock at the door. It was his next-door neighbor, Molly, a petite brunette with a penchant for wearing tight-fitting jeans and low cut blouses. He'd spoken to her twice since moving into his apartment.

"Hi." She flashed a wide a smile as she waved a section of the newspaper. "Have you seen it?" She pointed to the photo and article about his dancing and handed it to him.

"No, I haven't." He brushed his hair with his hand and took a moment to read it. "They made me out to be a better dancer than I really am." He chuckled. "Now I know how it feels to get your fifteen minutes of fame."

"It's a great write up. I'll bet you'll be getting a lot of attention the next time you show up at one of the dances." She paused and said not too shyly, "If you ever need someone to practice your steps, I'll be glad to be your partner. Just knock on my door. Well, gotta run. I'm late for work." She turned and rushed toward the parking lot.

"Thanks." He waved to her. He closed the door just as the phone rang.

"Did you read the article in the paper?" Ramona said the moment he answered.

"Yes, my neighbor was nice enough to show it to me."

"Well, we put it up on the bulletin board. The photo of us doing the foxtrot makes you look like a real pro. By the way, I just got off the phone with Julia. She hadn't read it yet, but said she was really proud of you."

"Did … she say anything else?"

"No, but she sounded a little down, which is understandable considering everything that's happened the past few days." Brief pause. "I see you're scheduled for an eleven o'clock lesson. Why don't you come early and we can talk some more?"

He was about to cancel it, but changed his mind. Ramona had always been supportive and he wanted to break it to her in person—that he had decided to move back to Florida. "Okay, Ramona. See you soon."

•　　　•　　　•

When Marco walked in the studio, teachers and students alike rushed to congratulate him. It wasn't every day that one of the students made the front page of the newspaper. Ramona waved the article in the air and gave him a hug.

They took a seat at one of the tables. "So how does it feel? Everybody has been talking about you. In fact, we got a few calls already from women who read the article and want to sign up for lessons. One of them said she wanted to meet you. Isn't that great?"

Marco forced a smile. "To be honest, I'm not used to getting so much attention. But if it helps to bring in more students, I'm all for it." He became serious. "Look, before we get started, I want to tell you how much I've enjoyed taking lessons from you. Both you and Julia have taught me so much and I know that I'm going to miss coming to the studio."

A confused look filled her face. "You sound like you won't be taking lessons anymore."

"I'm moving back to Miami." He looked down for a second. "My life is complicated. I wish I could explain. It's … rather personal."

"When do you plan to leave?"

"I'm not sure." He gave a small shrug. "Maybe tomorrow or the day after."

Ramona studied him for a moment. "You said it was personal and I may be out of line for saying this. Does Julia have anything do with it?"

"How did you know?" he said after a silence.

"Call it a woman's intuition. I could tell by the way you talked about her and the way she talked about you that something was going on, but I didn't know what, exactly."

Marco leaned back and tapped his temple with his forefinger. "You may as well know the truth. I like Julia. I like her a lot, and for a while I thought we had something between us … a special bond that went beyond teacher and student. I'll admit I fell in love with her, and I thought the feeling was mutual. But then when she told me she and Max were getting back together, well, I knew there was no point staying in Tucson. Not when I had important things to take care of back in Florida."

"For what it's worth, I think Julia is making a mistake. Are you sure you don't want to give it a couple of weeks? She might change her mind, you know. If you ask me the only reason she's going back to him is because she can depend on him during the difficult weeks and months to come."

"Funny you should say that because Julia said something similar when she explained why she couldn't see me anymore. Not that it matters. I've made up my mind and I just want to put this whole thing behind me." He didn't want her to feel sorry for him and he half-smiled. "I'll be okay. And even if I should get into a funk, I'll put on my dancing shoes and go dancing. I'm sure they have a lot of studios in South Florida." He became serious again. "I wrote Julia a letter. I was going to mail it to her, but since I'm here, can you give it to her the next time you see her?" He reached into his back pants pocket, then handed the envelope to Ramona.

"Sure, I'll be glad to. I may see her later tonight or tomorrow." She stood up. "Well, are you ready for your last lesson?"

"Let's do it." He forced a smile as he led the way to the center of the floor.

•   •   •

Back in his apartment, Marco began to have second thoughts about the letter. Maybe he should have mailed it after he got to Florida. What would Julia think if Ramona just handed it to her as though she were a go-between? The last thing he needed was for Julia to think he was trying to use Ramona's friendship to make her change her mind. After a moment, he called the studio and asked to speak with Ramona.

"She had an emergency with one of her kids and left a few minutes ago," said a woman who answered. "Would you care to leave a message?"

Marco thought about it for a second. "Just tell her Marco Anissi called. Maybe I'll try her later."

He had a lot on his mind, besides what Julia would or would not think after reading his letter. In a way he felt foolish, to have come all this way for nothing. But he didn't want to dwell on it, not when he had phone calls to make, and suitcases to pack.

The first call: to his sister who was surprised to hear from him. "Is everything okay?" she asked.

He closed his eyes for a second and let out a sigh. "I'm moving back to Florida. I hate to say it, but it was a mistake for me to come here."

"I'm so relieved to hear that. You don't know how many times I wanted to get on a plane to Tucson and bring you back with me. How soon do you plan to leave?"

"Tomorrow morning. Can you do me a favor? Can you please call Dr. Goldstein? He called a couple of days ago, but I wasn't able to speak with him. If he wants to reschedule my surgery, that's fine with me. I might as well get it over with."

"I'll take care of everything." Her voice softened, and she said, "Maybe I'll cook something special for you when you arrive, something you haven't had in a long time, like Mom's polenta with sausage and mushrooms."

"I'd like that." Marco gave her his itinerary for the three and a half day drive to Florida. At her insistence he promised to call when he reached the halfway point near Houston. When he hung up, he was glad she hadn't pressed for details about Julia. He was still reeling from yesterday's conversation with her and wasn't ready to hear *I told you so* from his sister or anyone else.

He spent the rest of the day packing and going over a to-do list: close bank account, drop off some items at the Goodwill bin, notify the phone company, call Tracy at the restaurant.

When he picked up his dancing shoes and placed them in a box, a rush of memories filled his brain. He sat down to record some thoughts.

Right now, I feel more numb than sad as I think about Julia. My last conversation with her plays in my mind over and over, like an old record where the needle gets stuck in a groove. It's still hard for me to believe, to accept that she doesn't want me in her life. In a way I feel like a fool—for believing that Susan had reached out to me—for listening to Professor Rangan—and especially for coming here thinking she'd fall in love with me the moment we met. The sooner I leave this city, the sooner I can begin to put it all behind me, even the dancing. It would be hard to enter a studio, any studio, and not think of Julia. Maybe I'll donate my shoes or maybe I'll hang on to them as a reminder of a lesson I thought I had learned years ago. That life is not fair. No one is promised a happy ending. I should know that better than anyone.

Tomorrow, I'll leave as early as possible and I won't look back. Too many reminders of what might have been. I'm sorry Susan, wherever you are, but I gave it my best.

17

I N THE MORNING, just before hitting the road, Marco wondered if Ramona had given his letter to Julia. In hindsight, he should have waited a week or two before writing it. If he had, he might have written it differently. He might have told her that he loved her and hoped they could stay in touch, or maybe— He stopped in mid-thought. There would be time enough for regrets and perhaps a few tears, but not for a while, not for a long while.

By eleven o'clock he was on I-10, well into the state of New Mexico. The sign up ahead said Las Cruces 40 miles. A half hour later another sign read Historic Mesilla. He took the exit, pulled into the nearest gas station and got out to stretch his legs and fill up the tank. Back in his car, he drove slowly into the heart of the village: an old Spanish plaza surrounded by adobe buildings dating back to the 1840s. Under different circumstances he might have taken the time to walk the streets, browse through some shops, and maybe eat at the Double Eagle Restaurant. According to a flyer he'd picked up at the gas station, the place was haunted by the ghosts of young lovers who had been tragically murdered in one of the rooms.

He followed the road that led back to the freeway and slowed to enter the on-ramp. When his phone rang he waited a few seconds before answering it.

The caller had hung up. He recognized Julia's number and got off at the next exit.

He pulled over behind a red pickup with a large sign on its side that said CHILES FROM HATCH, N.M.

She'd left a voice mail message. "Hi Marco," she said, her tone weary. "Ramona dropped by my apartment early this morning and gave me your letter. I wish you had told me all of this earlier. It explains a lot. As you can imagine, I'm very confused right now and I wish I knew what to do." A long pause, followed by a heavy sigh. "I'm sorry, I shouldn't have called." Her voice trailed off.

Marco sat in his car for the longest time. He felt torn between calling her back and continuing on. He leaned back on the headrest and closed his eyes, letting his mind drift freely for almost a minute. Suddenly the phone rang. It was Julia. He held his breath for a moment. "Hello," he said, exhaling slowly.

"I'm … not sure why I'm calling," she said after an awkward pause. "If you played back my message, you'll know that I'm struggling to make sense of your letter. I don't believe in the occult or whatever you want to call it, but I have to admit that maybe part of what you said was true. I mean, how else can you explain why I've had this nagging feeling that we've met before? By the way, I was never told about the donor's identity, except that it was someone who had died in a car accident."

"I should've been honest with you from the very beginning. Would it have made a difference?" He lifted his shoulders. "The truth is, I was afraid of what you might think. What guy in his right mind would drive across the country to meet a girl about whom he knew very little? I took a big gamble, Julia, and if I had it to do over again I'm not sure if I would. Not that it really matters. Right now I'm near Las Cruces on my way back to Miami."

"When Ramona told me you were leaving town, I had this strange sensation, almost like a panic attack. It was good that Ramona was here because she stayed with me until it passed. I don't know why but I'm having mixed feelings … about everything, and I'm scared."

"What are you afraid of?"

A long silence. "Before, when you asked if I was in love with Max, I wasn't entirely truthful. He's been a good friend, but I'm not in love with him. I feared being alone if the worst were to happen, and so I agreed to go back to him. I know it's a poor reason to be with someone but …"

"No need to explain. If I were in your position, I'd probably do the same. The question is, what do you want to do? I have a long drive ahead of me, but if there's a reason to turn back I would." He paused for a second. "Is there … a reason for me to return?"

She hesitated before answering. "You're putting me on the spot, but I guess the answer is yes."

"Are you sure?"

"Yes," she said, stretching the word for emphasis. "We have a lot to talk about and I'd rather do it in person."

He smiled. "That's all I wanted to hear. I'll be there in a few hours."

He had barely hung up when his sister's face popped into his head. He dreaded having to explain why he had to go back to Tucson.

Later, as he neared the New Mexico-Arizona border, he spotted a rest stop just ahead and he slowed to make the exit. Might as well get it over with. He parked at the far end of the lot, away from other cars, then dialed Angela's number.

She answered on the second ring. "I didn't expect to hear from you so soon. Are you okay?"

"Look, Sis, I know you won't agree with me, but something came up and I have to get back to Tucson. I was on the road in New Mexico when—"

"Don't tell me." She let out an audible sigh. "If it's about Julia, I don't want to hear it."

"You might as well know the truth. I'm in love with her and she wants to see me, to talk things over. This is the first time she's put it that way. I want us to have a chance, maybe the only chance we'll ever have."

"Marco, listen to me. Your tumor is like a ticking bomb and there is no time to waste. Does she even know about it?" She paused. "Oh, Marco, this is worse than I thought."

"I wanted to tell her but with her being so sick, well, it didn't make any sense. But things are different now and I know that I have to tell her something. Right now, the only thing I want to do is hurry back to see her, to find out where I stand. I don't think I have any choice. For my peace of mind I have to know if Susan's spirit really is playing a part in all of this. I'm sorry, Sis, but I have to follow my heart."

Angela didn't say anything for a long moment. "Okay, Marco, I see that I'm wasting my breath. I can't talk you out of it. But please do me a favor. Don't let this thing cloud your thinking any more than it already has. Do what you have to do, and for God's sake tell her about your tumor. If she really cares about you the way you think she does, she'll understand that you can't keep putting the surgery off indefinitely."

Marco nodded as he said goodbye. Her last comment left him feeling a bit down, but he got over it by the time he got back on the road. Julia was the only thing on his mind and he pressed the accelerator to gain a few extra minutes.

18

W HEN MARCO PULLED INTO Julia's complex, a queasiness in his stomach made him wonder if he was doing the right thing. Doubts crept into his brain and for a brief moment he wanted to turn the car around. Then he saw her step onto the balcony, almost as though she knew he'd show up at that very moment. He waved, parked his car and strode up to the apartment.

Julia greeted him with an awkward kiss on the cheek. "You must be exhausted after being on the road for so long. Have a seat while I pour us some wine."

He smiled. "I could use a glass." He crossed the room and sat on the couch. On the coffee table lay the article that had appeared in the newspaper. "I see you read what they wrote about me."

"It was a great write-up." She started to laugh. "I hope you enjoyed your unexpected moment of fame." Holding two wine-filled glasses she joined him on the couch.

Marco reached for one and they raised them simultaneously. "To fate and destiny," he toasted. "May they bring us peace and happiness." They clicked their glasses, then took a quick sip.

Julia half-smiled. "I want you to know that I'm not an impulsive person by nature and it was out of character for me to call you. But I'm glad I did. After we hung up I wanted to take a nap but I couldn't. My mind was filled with all sorts of thoughts … about you, about me, about whether we were doing the right thing." She leaned back and closed her eyes for a second.

Marco sipped on his wine. "Since we're being honest, I have to admit I thought I'd never hear from you again. Almost three hundred miles away the only thing on my mind was to get to Miami, resume my old life, maybe enroll at the university." He stared at her for a long moment as though in disbelief that she really wanted to see him.

"Tell me about Susan." Julia placed her hand over his. "In your letter you mentioned she was your fiancée. What was she like?"

Marco's mind raced through a thousand memories from the day they met in their junior year of college to the day he proposed to her on the steps of the Spanish Monastery—four months before the accident. He let out a long, wistful sigh. "Susan was unlike any girl I had ever met before: kind of shy, smart, and extremely inquisitive. What I liked most about her was her sense of compassion. She wanted to make a difference in the world and looked forward to being a social worker or maybe a counselor for troubled teenagers. And she loved to read, especially books by writers who inspired her, like Albert Camus and her favorite Kahlil Gibran." He choked up and paused for a moment. "We were seniors and planned to marry right after graduation."

"I'm sorry. I shouldn't have asked."

"It's okay. In fact I'm glad you did. It's better that you know about her and why I felt certain she had reached out to me the day I crashed into the pole. I just knew I had to meet you." He chuckled. "Though I didn't imagine I would have to travel half-way across the country."

She squeezed his hand. "A few days ago, I might have dismissed it all as just a coincidence: the unexplainable feeling that I had met you before, my love of Kahlil Gibran. It all meant something, didn't it?"

He nodded. "Just like your perfume—Casmir. Susan's favorite. And even the dancing. I had almost forgotten that one day while we were at a friend's wedding, a band started to play an old Frank Sinatra song and we stepped onto the floor. In the middle of the dance Susan suggested that we take lessons, a hobby we could enjoy together for the rest of our lives. We were kind of broke at the time, so we never did, but she brought it up again when we accidentally tuned in to a ballroom dance competition on public television."

"I envy you, Marco … the way you talk about her. She was lucky to have had you in her life if only for a brief period. How I wish I could have been so fortunate. When I got married, I was young and naïve. I thought that Andrew would be my soul mate with whom I would grow old … who would love me in sickness and in health." She sighed.

"When we found out that my heart was giving out on me, he couldn't handle it, the uncertainty of it all. Not even after I had my transplant. He eventually left me and I had no choice but to move forward … alone. When my friend Ramona called one day to say they needed an experienced teacher for their advanced students, I jumped at the chance. I took the first plane to Tucson. So now you know how I wound up here. I have no regrets even though I miss Florida. I just wish I could go back there more often."

Marco took a long sip of wine. "Can you put on some music … the CD by Eva Cassidy? The one you played the last time I was here?"

"Sure. It's one of my favorites." She got up, pulled out the disk and slipped it into the player. Soon, Eva's soft, mesmerizing voice filled the room. Julia closed her eyes as she moved her head to the rhythm of the music. A second later, Marco stood up, and extended his hand. "May I have this dance?"

She nodded, smiling. It was a slow song, which made it easy for her to follow him without getting overexerted. When it ended Marco moved closer and kissed her, gently at first and then passionately. They held each other for a long moment.

"Are we doing the right thing?" she blurted. "I mean, it's all happening so fast."

He looked into her soft brown eyes. "I don't know. But I'm not worried about it. I don't want to over analyze what is happening, especially now. Just a few hours ago I thought I'd never see you again, that I'd lost you forever. And here we are in each other's arms. Let's just enjoy the moment."

"You're right. We can't worry about the future. I should know better than anyone." She hesitated. "But there is one thing though, that we need to discuss. I don't know how to say this …"

"What? What is it?"

"Let's sit down." She took his hand and they ambled back to the couch.

Marco took a sip of wine and she did the same. Finally, Julia came right out with it. "I understand why you felt that you had to meet me, but I have to know who you see, who you think of when we're together. Just now, were you kissing Susan or were you kissing me? What I'm trying to say is that I don't want to live in her shadow. I want you to love me for who I am, not for who you want me to be. There's a good chance I'll have another transplant, which means I'll no longer have Susan's heart. Have you thought about that?"

Marco was silent for a long while. "There isn't anything you said that I haven't thought about. When I left Florida I had mixed emotions because of the possibility you might turn out to be somebody with whom I'd have nothing in common. But it was a gamble I was willing to take. And I'm glad I did. From the day we met, I was drawn to you. Sure, in the beginning it was because of Susan. But later as I got to know you, I had fantasies that had nothing to do with her. Don't you see? Susan's spirit was a kind of vehicle for me to get to know you and yes, to fall in love. So to answer your question, the woman I kissed was you, definitely you."

Julia nodded and released a slow sigh. "I hope you understand why I had to hear you say that."

He smiled, then became serious. "Now, I have question for you. Have you thought about what you're going to tell Max?"

"I called him, just moments before you got here. He didn't take it very well."

"What did you tell him?"

"The truth … that I had changed my mind about getting back together. I didn't tell him about you because he wouldn't understand. He wanted to come over to discuss it but I told him I was tired and planned to go to bed early. In a way I feel bad because he's been so good to me. He cared about me in a way my husband never really did." She took a deep breath and reached for her wine. "You must be hungry. We can order a pizza or I can make us a couple of sandwiches."

He smiled. "Pizza sounds good. I'll order it. What would you like on it?"

A knock came at the door. She got up to answer it. It was Max. "I need to speak to you."

She hesitated, then allowed him to enter.

"Well, I know you two need to talk." Marco got up. Under the circumstances, he didn't know what else to say. "I'll call you later." Julia nodded and waited for him to leave.

Marco's shoulders drooped as he walked back to his car. Maybe he should have stayed. Maybe Julia *expected* him to stay. Maybe … He shook his head. No point worrying about it. He cranked the engine and looked at his watch. If he hurried he might find his old apartment still available. If so, he'd move back in for a month or two, or until he and Julia could sort things out. Later, he might even move in with her. The thought of it made him smile.

Marco waited almost an hour before calling Julia.

"Yes, he left a few minutes ago." She sounded tense. "It wasn't easy for me … to tell him that I wasn't in love with him."

"I'm sorry. After everything you've told me about him, I know how you must feel." He hesitated. "I can come over … unless you think it's too late or you're feeling tired."

"I am kind of tired. But I do want to see you, if only for a few minutes."

"You sure?"

"Uh-huh. I'll be waiting for you."

•   •   •

"You didn't tell me what you like on your pizza," Marco said the moment Julia opened the door. "So I went ahead and ordered my favorite: fresh garlic, anchovies and onions." He stepped inside and placed the box on the dining table along with a bottle of Chianti.

Julia started to frown. "Fresh garlic and anchovies? Is that an Italian thing?"

"It was my grandfather's favorite. I hope you like it." He grinned as he opened the box and waited for Julia's reaction.

She laughed. The large New York style pizza was topped with fresh basil, pepperoni, mushrooms and green peppers. "You sure had me going there for a while. Not that I don't like anchovies and garlic. Just not on my pizza."

Marco opened the bottle of wine and poured some into two glasses while Julia set the table. He lit a long-tapered candle before they sat down to eat. "I want you to know I have a weakness for pizza, especially with pepperoni."

She smiled. "I'm glad you brought it." She took a sip of wine. "And the Chianti is perfect."

"For me pizza is comfort food. Ever since I was a kid I always felt better after eating a slice or two. Even now if I'm feeling down for any reason, a good pizza seems to do the trick."

Their conversation remained light until they finished eating. "I don't know if I should admit this," Julia said during a lull. "After Max left, a sadness came over me and I didn't want to be alone. That's why I asked you to come over. I hope you understand."

Marco nodded. "Any regrets?"

A solemn, pensive look came over her. "Regrets, no. Fears, yes. I just pray that my heart will last long enough for us to enjoy each other. As you know I'm supposed to be on call twenty-four seven, waiting for a donor. I try to stay optimistic, but sometimes when I go to bed at night, I worry that I might not wake up." Brief pause. "I'm sorry I didn't mean to get heavy." She reached for her wine and took a long sip.

Marco did the same. After a moment he stood to leave. "It's getting late and you must really be tired."

"Where are you staying?"

"I was lucky to move back into my apartment where I can rent on a month to month basis like I did before."

She walked him to the door. "Maybe … maybe later we can make some other arrangements."

He smiled. "I'd like that. Let's talk about it when I see you again … like tomorrow?"

She nodded, then closed her eyes as he cocked his head and brought his lips to hers. They savored each other for a long moment until he broke away. "I'll call you in the morning."

Later, just before going to bed, Marco played the day's events over in his mind and wrote in his journal.

My head is still spinning and I'm in a pleasant state of shock. Here I thought I'd never hear from Julia again and the next moment I get a call from her saying she wants to see me. I was 300 miles away, with no other thought than to get back to Florida as fast as I could. Finally, everything is falling into place. Julia knows all about Susan and the reason I felt compelled to meet the girl who had received her heart. I feel as though a burden has been lifted from my shoulders.

I am now free to concentrate on what promises to be a great relationship. But I know that things can change quickly, depending on whether or not Julia gets another transplant. No matter, she and I are together just as I had always imagined, and for that I am grateful.

19

THE NEXT MORNING, Marco called Julia and talked to her briefly. She sounded groggy as though she'd just gotten out of bed. "Do you mind if we have a late breakfast or better yet an early lunch? After you left I fell asleep on the couch. When I awoke forty minutes later, I felt disoriented. I could feel my heart pounding harder than usual. Had to stay up for a couple of hours before going to bed."

"Lunch would be fine. But if you need more time …"

"I'll be okay. I've gone through this before." Brief pause. "I'll prepare something light for us. Maybe a salad or some BLT sandwiches."

"Salad sounds good to me. Heck, I could even go for the leftover pizza with an egg on top." He chuckled. "Yes, it's an Italian thing. I'll see you between eleven-thirty and twelve."

He had the morning to kill and used the time to call Tracy at the Greek restaurant to let her know he'd be available. Then he drove to the studio to chat with Ramona. She flashed a big smile and rushed over to greet him. "I thought you had left town."

"I did. I got as far as New Mexico." He grinned, anxious to share the good news. "That's where I got the call from Julia. She wanted me to come back. I was stunned, to say the least. Here I thought that I'd never hear from her again, much less see her, and the next moment, I'm driving back to Tucson."

"I don't know what to say. Of course I'm happy for you, but what about Max? I thought—"

"Max is out of the picture. It's a long story. Maybe Julia can explain it better than I can. Right now I'm just happy to be back. I even had to pinch myself to make sure it wasn't a dream."

"You really are in love with her, aren't you?"

He nodded. "I am, but it's more than that. After years of dating all the wrong girls, I never thought I'd find someone like Julia. Someone who is right for me in almost every way." He smiled. "I felt a connection with her the moment I met her."

"You had a serious expression on your face that day. Later, when Julia told me she would be your teacher, I was really surprised considering she only took experienced dancers. Looking back, I can see that maybe she felt as you did, and with both of you being from Florida, well …" She grinned. "I'm just glad you're back. And if you want my opinion, I think the two of you make a great couple."

Though he hadn't sought Ramona's approval, her words had a wonderful ring. He couldn't wait to tell Julia.

"I'm supposed to be at Julia's in half an hour." He stepped back. "Gotta run. Why don't we schedule a lesson for tomorrow, say around one?"

"Make it two o'clock. I have a new student at one—a doctor, no less. He's supposed to be one of the best surgeons in town."

"I'll see you then." He gave her a quick hug and hurried out of the studio.

Julia's eyes sparkled when Marco walked in holding a yellow rose. He gave her a quick kiss and glanced at the table: white plates on black place mats, a lit candle, and a large bowl of salad. Next to it, an opened bottle of wine from the night before.

"Yellow is my favorite. Thank you." She smelled it, then placed it on the table near the candle. "Hope you're hungry. I made one of my favorite salads." She laughed. "Not really. I put something together with whatever I had in the fridge."

They sat down and looked at each other. "I saw Ramona at the studio, just before coming here." He poured some wine into their glasses, then continued. "She was surprised to see me, as you can imagine."

Julia reached for the salad bowl and served a generous amount on each plate. "Did you tell her about us?"

"I did." Marco picked up a fork and studied the salad: large spinach leaves, crisp bacon bits, chopped walnuts, topped with crumbled feta and just the right amount of vinaigrette. "Interesting combination." He put a forkful in his mouth. "Very good."

"I'm glad you like it." She took a sip of wine. "So, what did you tell Ramona?"

"I told her about your phone call and that I came back to be with the girl I fell in love with. I didn't give her any details because I figured you'd want to tell her yourself."

He paused. "Just as I was about to leave she said something I didn't expect her to say." He reached for his wine.

"What did she say?"

Marco grinned. "That we made a great couple." He lifted his glass and she lifted hers. "To the great couple we are meant to be."

After lunch they took a stroll along a winding path that led to a large fountain near the main entrance. "I'm getting a little tired," she said. "The doctor wants me to walk a little every day, but not to overdo it. Let's take a break." They sat on a bench and watched sparrows flying in and out of the fountain. Their chirping sounds complemented the steady sound of the water that splashed all around them.

He reached for her hand. "There's something I need to tell you." He hesitated, not quite sure how to explain that he, too, faced an uncertain future. He wondered if he could avoid giving details. Not just about his tumor but about the surgery he'd called off just to be back in town. Would she understand? Or would she recoil and not want to see him anymore? His phone rang, causing him to flinch. It was Tracy from the restaurant, wanting to know if he could work the rest of the day and evening.

"I don't know if I can make it." He turned away from Julia. "I had already made plans to—"

"It's a big celebration for a Greek couple who just got engaged. I'll pay you extra and you can leave a little early if you want."

"Let me think about it. I'll call you right back." Tracy's timing was difficult to ignore. He took it as a sign that maybe he should wait a day or two before telling Julia about his medical condition. He turned to Julia. "That was Tracy, the manager from the Greek restaurant where I've worked a couple of times. She needed an extra cook to help out for the rest of the day."

"I think you should go. I over did it by staying up late last night and planned on turning in early. I'll be okay."

"You sure? I mean, I'd rather stay with you and maybe do something fun like go for a drive or watch a video."

She nodded. "The last thing I want is for you to rearrange your life or your schedule just to be with me. Giving each other space, whether it be for an afternoon or a day can be a good thing, you know." She smiled. "We'll be that much more eager to see each other."

"Well, when you put it that way …" They got up and walked back to the apartment.

"I'll call you later tonight when I get home from work." He kissed her and hurried down the stairs.

20

D AYS LATER, MARCO STILL HADN'T TOLD Julia about his tumor, nor had he called Angela. In between seeing Julia and working at the restaurant he continued to write in his journal. He'd left Julia's apartment less than an hour ago and scribbled a few lines.

For the first time, Julia admitted that she had a fear of physical intimacy, and for a very good reason. Her doctor had warned her not to engage in strenuous physical activity, which explained why she seemed reluctant to lie in bed with me, and why she wasn't ready for us to live together.

He continued with a call he got from Tracy at the restaurant.

Tracy surprised me today when she offered me a full-time job as an assistant chef. I was flattered that she thought so highly of my cooking skills. I told her I'd think it over. But a full-time job would mean less time with Julia. What if her condition should worsen? She'll need me on a moment's notice. Right now I enjoy the flexibility of working part-time and seeing Julia as often as I can. Though I need the money, I feel I have no choice but to tell Tracy that I can't accept her offer. She's been good to me and deserves to know the reason. I'll confide in her the next time I see her.

• • •

The next day, Marco got up earlier than usual. He had to pick up Julia for an 8:00 a.m. appointment. On his way to her apartment his phone rang. He waited a few seconds before answering it.

"I hadn't heard from you in a while," Angela said. "How are you doing?"

He hesitated for a moment. "I meant to call you, but a lot has happened and I haven't had time to—"

"What did she have to say when you told her about your tumor?"

"Can I call you back later? I'm on my way to pick up Julia to take her to the doctor. We can talk better after I bring her back home in a couple of hours."

"You haven't told her, have you?"

Marco sighed. "I tried to, and then I just kept putting it off. I know what you're going to say and you're right. The thing is, she and I are getting along so well. I didn't want to do anything to spoil it. When I drove back to see her I had a lot of misgivings, not knowing what to expect. But as it turned out we realized we need each other, maybe for different reasons, not that it matters. We're in love, Sis. Can't you be happy for us?"

"Listen, Marco. You have no time to lose. If this girl loves you the way you think she does, she'll understand. Talk to her and explain you have a pressing medical condition that cannot be ignored. She's entitled to know the truth. She might surprise you and offer to help in whatever way she can. But you won't know unless you talk to her. Please, Marco, do it and do it soon."

Marco stopped at a light and stared at a young, dark-haired woman stepping off the curb. She reminded him of Julia. For a second their eyes met as she walked directly in front of him. The light turned green. "Julia means everything to me. I wouldn't want to lose her," he said after a pause. "To tell you the truth, I've avoided saying anything because I feared she'd back away, especially if the operation didn't go well. Sometimes it's easier to pretend that everything is fine, which I know it isn't. I'm aware that I can't go on pretending forever." He let out a sigh. "I'll talk to her. But not today. She may be getting some more bad news from the doctor and I wouldn't want to add to that."

"I understand, but don't put it off. And for God's sake let me know what you're doing. When Dr. Goldstein called me this morning, I didn't know what to tell him. He's concerned that you're not taking this as seriously as you should. He's right, of course. Please do what you have to do and get back here as soon as you can."

Angela made a lot of sense. He hung up after assuring her that he'd keep her posted, though he really didn't know how or when he'd tell Julia about his tumor.

In the evening, just before going to bed, Marco wrote a quick note in his journal.

After talking to Angela, I know I have no choice but to speak to Julia about my tumor. I'll figure out a way to skip some of the details. I wouldn't want to alarm her. Then when the time is right, I'll tell her everything. Well, maybe not everything. Just enough to let her know I take my condition seriously despite what my sister and others may think.

21

North Miami

"THE BODY IS A VESSEL that contains not one soul but many," Professor Rangan said. He spoke with a lilting voice that had a mesmerizing effect on his listeners—mostly grad students and Eastern religion devotees. "There is a dominant soul, which is the one that most organized religions recognize, and rightfully so. But there are others, parts of a soul if you will, that inhabit our organs, especially our hearts. They are no less significant because collectively, they complement the dominant soul, preparing it perhaps for a better journey to the other side."

A young woman in the front row raised her hand. "I'm a devout Christian and I'm not sure I can accept what you are suggesting. I mean, about the heart possessing part of one's soul. I've always been taught to believe that a body has only one soul and when you die, it leaves the body and goes to Heaven."

Professor Rangan took a moment to respond. "First of all, this is a theory that's been around for many centuries, mostly in the East. Of course, like most spiritual theories, one has to have a certain amount of faith to accept it. Just as you do with other ideas, to include the resurrection of Christ." He smiled at her. "Christianity and other religions, you must understand, are like warm, fuzzy blankets. They are there mostly to provide comfort, which all of us need at different stages of our lives. I'm not trying to make light of your faith, but you have to remember that long before Christianity came along, there were many other beliefs that, at the time, were considered valid just as Christianity is now considered to be. Who is to say that some of these same beliefs are obsolete, or even irrelevant?"

He paused, then added. "It's not what happens to us when we die or whether there is one soul or many. It really doesn't matter, and that's the beauty of it. Don't you see? It's the journey that counts."

He glanced at the clock on the wall. "Well, I see we're out of time. We'll continue on Monday. Have a safe and happy weekend." He started to collect his papers when Angela, who had been sitting in the back of the room, walked up to the podium. "I'm Angela Newport, Marco Anissi's sister. I wonder if I could speak to you for a moment."

He hesitated. "I have a visitor waiting for me at my office, but we can talk on the way. How is Marco?"

"Not well, I'm afraid. That's what I want to talk to you about." They made their way out of the classroom, down a short hall, then exited the building. "I know he met with you shortly after he got out of the hospital. Afterward, he decided to look for the girl who had received his fiancée's heart. He eventually found her in Tucson, Arizona. He fell in love with her as you might imagine. Meanwhile, one of his doctors had taken a second look at his brain scan and thought Marco might have a tumor. To get to the point, Marco came back and they verified he did have a tumor, which doctors said was operable, thank God."

"Did he have the surgery?"

"That's the problem. He keeps putting if off. It turns out that Julia, the woman who received his fiancée's heart, is beginning to reject it. So now, Marco doesn't want to leave her while she waits for another transplant. To make matters worse, he hasn't told her about his tumor. I talked to him yesterday and he promised he would, but I'm not sure that he will. He doesn't want to upset her, though I think she would probably encourage him to have the surgery. His doctor is afraid that if he waits too long, it may be too late."

They walked around a group of students handing out fliers for an anti-war protest and cut across a grassy area. Professor Rangan turned to Angela. "I'm not sure I understand why you came to see me. But if I can help in any way, I'll be more than happy to do so."

She half-smiled. "So far I've had no luck in convincing Marco that he must come back for the surgery. I'm just his big sister who he can ignore again and again. I know he respects you, especially because he believes in your metaphysical theories or whatever you call them. If it's not too much to ask, can you speak to him—just to let him know you're concerned about him? He'll know of course that I talked to you, but that's okay."

"In a way I feel partly responsible that he had to move so far away because of something I said. Marco was a good student and I'm sorry he never completed his studies." He nodded. "Sure, I'll be glad to help."

Angela handed him a piece of paper with Marco's phone number. "Thank you. I just know you'll have better luck than I did."

•   •   •

"Professor Rangan, what a surprise," Marco said the moment he answered the phone. "How did you get my number?"

"Look, Marco. I won't waste your time or mine. I'm calling because your sister is worried about you. She came to see me and told me everything. About Julia, about your tumor, and the surgery you keep putting off."

"My sister had no right to discuss this with you, but since she did all I can say is I'm doing the best I can."

"I know you are. And I know you have your reasons for not wanting to have your surgery right now. But you're gambling with your life, Marco. You know that, don't you? I told your sister I feel partly responsible for the way things turned out. That's why I'm asking you to come home and have the surgery as soon as possible."

"I understand what you're saying, but I still have some things to resolve with Julia before I return to Miami. I need some more time."

Rangan was silent for a moment. "I wasn't going to say this, but if what your sister said is true—about Julia needing another transplant—it's going to change her in a way that you may not expect."

Marco gripped the phone. "What do you mean?'

"I'm saying that Susan's spirit … what initially drew you to Julia will cease to exist the moment she gets a new heart. Julia may not even be aware of it, but part of her, maybe the part that you fell in love with, will no longer be there. The chemistry between the two of you will most certainly be altered, which means you may not feel the same about her as you did in the beginning."

"But we love each other. There's nothing in the world that will make me change the way I feel about her. And I'm sure she would say that about me."

Professor Rangan released an exasperated sigh. "What I'm trying to say is that your future with her is uncertain and you might as well come home to have the surgery. You have much more to gain than to lose. That's how you have to look at it."

Marco considered it for a moment. "I appreciate your concern, Professor Rangan, and I know you mean well." He finished with a few awkward words that left him feeling a little down, but not for long. He'd made plans to take Julia for a drive to Mount Lemmon and he couldn't wait to see her.

22

T HE NEXT DAY, Marco walked into Julia's apartment carrying a bag full of groceries. He gave her a quick peck on the lips, then set the bag on the kitchen counter. "I got most of the things on your list, except for the nicoise olives. They're hard to find in this town. Someone told me about a gourmet store at La Encantada Mall that carries them. I'll drop by there tomorrow if I get a chance."

"I really appreciate you doing this for me. Maybe next time I'll go with you. It'll be fun shopping together. We've never done that."

He smiled. "Yes, it would be a lot of fun. It's all about building memories, you know. One after the other. From silly things to simple ordinary things like going to see a movie or eating at a favorite restaurant." He glanced at the clock on the wall. "I can't stay too long. Got to be at the restaurant in less than an hour. Tracy needed some help for a big group coming in for an early lunch."

"The way she keeps calling you, I wouldn't be surprised if she offered you a full-time job."

He cleared his throat. "That would be great. But then I wouldn't be able to see you as often."

The phone rang. She crossed the room to answer it. "Thank you," she said after holding her breath. She sniffled and took a moment to compose herself.

"Are you okay?" He moved closer.

"That was Dr. Levine, the transplant coordinator. He said that a heart belonging to a woman in a coma would soon become available. I have a chance of being the recipient."

"That's great. But you don't seem that excited about it."

"He said the woman's husband was having second thoughts, despite the wishes of her children from a previous marriage."

Marco stared at her for a moment. "Well, it's still good news. We have to stay positive and pray that you have a chance. When will you know?"

"They expect to remove her life support within the next few days. Meanwhile Dr. Levine will stay in touch with the family." She crossed her arms and began to pace. "I need to do something, something to help take my mind away from all this, at least for a while." She stopped pacing. "I have an idea. When you leave, can you drop me off at the studio? I haven't been there since I collapsed. I'd love to see everyone. Ramona or one of the other teachers can bring me back home."

"I think it's a good idea. It'll do you good to be with old friends. I'll help you unpack the groceries and we can be on our way."

Later, he dropped Julia off at the studio. She stayed there for almost an hour.

Afterward, Ramona gave her a ride. They had a chance to talk, without the distraction of Julia's friends and students back at the studio.

"So, how is it going, with you and Marco?" Ramona asked.

Julia turned to her, smiling. "We're getting to know a lot about each other and I couldn't be happier. Of course, Max didn't take it well when I told him I couldn't see him anymore. I felt really bad about it. He's been such a good friend over the past few years. I do care about him, you know, but not in the same way I care about Marco." She leaned back on the headrest. "I don't mind telling you that for the first time since my husband left me, I'm in love, really in love. It feels wonderful."

"Well, being in love certainly agrees with you. I know Max was good to you but to be honest, I think you and Marco are a much better match." She laughed. "And he likes to dance. How cool is that?"

As they neared her apartment, Julia confided in Ramona about a possible donor. "I don't want to build up my hopes too much, but it's hard not to … especially now that Marco has come into my life."

"When will you know?"

"The doctor said it could be any day." She sighed. "I've been through this before and I know things can change quickly. Please say a prayer for me."

Ramona smiled. "I will. Call me if you feel like visiting the studio again." She dropped Julia off and waited for her to walk up the stairs.

23

Three days later

THE PHONE RANG just before 9:00 a.m. Julia recognized Dr. Levine's number and picked it up on the second ring. She took a deep breath. "Yes, I understand." Her lips quivered. "It won't be necessary. I'll … I'll be okay. Thank you for letting me know." Tears filled her eyes as she hung up the phone.

Marco called less than a minute later. He could tell she'd been crying. "What is it? Did you talk to the doctor?"

She sniffled a couple of times. "I won't be getting the transplant. At the last minute, the woman's family decided not to donate her heart."

"But why? What made them change their mind?"

"Does it matter? I'd rather put it behind me and pretend I never had a chance. It's easier for me to think that way otherwise I'll go crazy, or worse feel sorry for myself." Brief pause. "I need to do something … get some fresh air, maybe take a drive. Do you think we could go someplace where I don't have to think about anything heavy?"

"Say no more. See you in a few minutes."

When he pulled into the parking lot, he saw her standing on the balcony. She waved to him. "I'll be right down."

He met her at the foot of the stairs. "I'm so sorry," he whispered as he wrapped his arms around her.

"I'm a survivor, remember?" Her eyes were still red from crying. "So where are you taking me?" She attempted a smile.

He grinned. "You'll see. It's a place I've been to only once, but it's a nice drive. So, sit back and relax."

A moment later they were on Kolb heading south, then later still, on the highway to Nogales. When Marco asked if Dr. Levine had mentioned the possibility of another donor, Julia became quiet and shook her head. "If you don't mind, I'd rather not talk about it, at least for the rest of the day."

Just ahead, Marco spotted the exit sign for the San Xavier Mission, barely visible in the distance. "Have you been here before?" He slowed and put on his right turn signal.

A soft smile crossed her face. "I love this place. I came here when I first moved to Tucson and I always wanted to return. For some reason I never did."

He turned onto a winding road that led to the old church: an imposing white structure that looked like a monument to the past, when Spain ruled the territory and its native inhabitants. Partially surrounded by small homes and sparse desert landscape, the centuries-old church had recently been renovated. They parked in a large graveled lot and walked toward the building—past open huts with hand-painted signs that said: INDIAN FRY BREAD. INDIAN TACOS.

"Maybe later we can try the fry bread," Julia said with a hint of a smile.

"Sure. I had some the first time I came here. I liked it but it was way too much for me so I shared it with a tourist from Canada. He enjoyed it and ordered another one to take with him."

They paused in the middle of a patio that led to the church.

"Let's go inside for a moment." A serene look filled Julia's face as she stepped toward the large open doorway.

A sign near the entrance read:

Mission San Xavier del Bac was founded by Jesuit priest and explorer Father Eusebio Kino in 1692. The construction of the church began in 1783 under the direction of the Franciscans and was completed in 1797. The church continues to serve the Tohono O'odham, the native people of this land.

Julia made a quick sign of the cross and led the way to the front, crossed herself again and took a seat in one of the pews. Marco did the same and sat beside her, shutting out all negative thoughts and fears, if only temporarily. He gave her a minute as she bowed her head in prayer. A moment later they got up and stepped toward a reclining statue of San Francisco Xavier. Julia lit a candle and crossed herself again.

They left the church and strolled through the grounds, ending up in one of the patios facing a small mountain with a circular path that led to the top. They sat on a bench near a gray, crumbling statue whose rough-cut features barely resembled St. Francis of Assisi.

"I'm so glad you brought me here." Julia smiled. "This church … this place … there's something about it that gives me comfort in a way that I can't quite explain."

"I know what you mean. I feel the same. It would be nice to attend one of the Masses."

She nodded. "I'd like that. Maybe we could make a day of it and afterwards have a picnic someplace close by … that is if I'm feeling up to it."

Marco squeezed her hand and smiled. A moment later an old woman in a long floral dress entered the patio and sat on a bench. She stared at them for a second, then pulled out a camera from her purse and asked, "Do you mind if I take your picture?"

Marco and Julia looked at each other. "Sure, if you want." Marco gave a small shrug.

The woman snapped a quick photo and put the camera away. "I saw you as you were walking to the mission and later as you sat in the church. I don't know why but you reminded me of Alfred and me. We were about the same age as you two when we met. We ran away to get married. I was Catholic and he wasn't." She paused. "In those days, you had to marry a Catholic. Nowadays it doesn't matter that much, which I guess is a good thing if you happen to fall in love with someone outside your faith.

"He passed away six months ago," she said after a pause.

"I'm sorry," Julia said softly.

"That's okay." She said with a gleam in her eye. "He gave me a gift of fond memories that will forever stay in my heart. We had a wonderful life and I have no regrets." She smiled. "Well, maybe just one. I wish we could have had more children."

"How many do you have?" Marco asked.

"Two. A son and a daughter. And now I'm fortunate to be a grandmother to six beautiful children." Her smile faded. "But they live far away in Montana and Colorado and I don't get to see them that often." She stood up. "Well, I didn't mean to intrude. If you'd like, I can send you a copy of the picture?"

Julia turned to Marco and then to the woman. "That's very nice of you." She scribbled her name and address on a piece of paper and handed it to her.

"Que dios los bendiga," the old woman said. "God bless you." She walked away and paused in mid step. "I can tell that you are truly in love with each other. The way Alfred and I were in love. If I may offer some advice. Cherish this moment, this hour because no one knows what the future will bring." There was a sadness in her eyes as she turned and hurried out of the patio.

"What an odd thing for her to say," Julia said. "It's almost as if she knew that our future was uncertain because of my failing heart."

Marco frowned. "I'm sure she meant well, but I wouldn't dwell on it." He changed the subject to lighten the mood. "Still interested in trying some Indian fry bread?"

Julia smiled. "Good idea." They left the patio and ambled toward the row of open huts where Indian women stood next to oil drum grills making fresh bread: ready-made dough, patted into the shape of a thick tortilla, then gently dropped into a kettle of hot oil.

A young boy and his little sister, playing near one of the huts, waved to them to get their attention. "Over here," he said, pointing to his mother's hut. "My mom makes the best Indian bread in the village."

Marco and Julia stepped up to the woman's hut. "One fry bread." He held up his forefinger. "With honey and cinnamon."

After tasting it, Julia said, "It's really good. Better than I thought it would be." They strode back to the car.

Marco nodded. "Maybe next time we'll try the Indian tacos."

They drove away from the mission, toward the main highway and to the road that led back to Julia's apartment. The little excursion had taken Julia's mind away from her troubles, at least for a while. That's all that mattered. For the rest of the day they pretended she'd never received the doctor's phone call.

24

T WO O'CLOCK IN THE MORNING. Unable to sleep, Marco got up and wrote in his journal.

For the first time I am afraid that Julia might not live long enough to receive a second transplant. But I must stay strong, as much for her as for myself. God help me. I don't know what I would do if she died alone. Tomorrow I will broach the subject again about moving in with her.

Though I had considered telling her about my tumor, I do not believe it would serve any purpose. She is still reeling from the doctor's phone call. No need to add to her worries.

•   •   •

"We've talked about this before, Marco," Julia said from across her kitchen table. "The truth is, I need my space ... to come to terms with what is happening to me. I don't want to have to depend on you simply because we're living in the same apartment. Let's give it a few more weeks and then—"

"It's the intimacy issue, isn't it? Look, I know it's awkward. What if I slept on the couch? It's not the best arrangement, but under the circumstances I think I can handle it." He grinned. "It would be nice to be able to serve you breakfast in bed. I make a killer omelet and buttermilk pancakes that are so light ... well, you'll just have to find out for yourself."

"Hmm ... breakfast in bed ... very tempting." She smiled, then reached to hold his hand. "Look, Marco I would like nothing better than to wake up every morning and see your smiling face. Maybe even help you cook breakfast. But it's too soon. Everything is happening so fast. Your letter, my breakup with Max and yesterday's phone call saying I won't be getting a transplant. It's just too much for me to handle. So, please Marco, give me a few more days, and I promise that when the time is right ..." She smiled. "I'll *insist* you pack your things and come right over. And no, you won't have to sleep on the couch."

Marco let out a sigh. "Okay, if that's the way you want it, then that's the way it will be. It'll give me something to look forward to. Just don't wait too long; otherwise I might think you've changed your mind." He glanced at his watch. "I've got a lesson with Ramona in twenty minutes. Don't want to be late." He got up, gave her a quick kiss and hurried out the door.

•　　•　　•

Before the lesson, Marco and Ramona took a moment to chat, mostly about Julia and her refusal to allow him to move in with her.

"She's being very stubborn about this, even though she knows she will eventually need someone to help her." He shook his head. "I backed off only because I didn't want to upset her. I mean, what choice did I have?"

"So, what is she going to do? Does she even have a chance of getting another transplant?"

"She's back on the waiting list, of course. But you know how that goes. It could be weeks, months before she hears anything." He sighed. "To be honest, I don't know if she'll last that long."

A pained look crossed Ramona's face. "I don't know what to say. I wish I could do something. Maybe I'll talk to her … woman to woman. I'll call her as soon as we're done with the lesson."

"Good idea, but if you have time, can you pay her a visit? She could use the company."

Ramona smiled. "I'll go see her during my lunch break."

"One more thing. Please don't mention we had this conversation. I wouldn't want her to think that I sent you, just to make her change her mind."

"Don't worry. I'll know how to handle it." She stood up. "Let's work on a new dance. You're a quick learner and I think it's time to try something a bit more challenging. Like the Viennese Waltz. It's fast, but very elegant."

He followed her to the corner of the floor, got into frame, then wrapped his arm around her waist.

•   •   •

Julia poured some tea into two cups and handed one to Ramona. They sat at the kitchen table.

"You've been talking to Marco." Julia took a quick sip of her tea. "Not that I mind, really. I'm just not used to having people feel sorry for me. I know he cares for me deeply and he's only trying to help. But I have to do things in my own way, in my own time."

Ramona nodded. "He's worried about you and so am I. It's only natural for the people who love you to want to do something. He thinks you're being stubborn and I have to agree. But seriously, I think you should reconsider his offer to move in with you. He's a great guy and you're lucky he came into your life."

Julia smiled. "Yes, I am very fortunate. Still, when I think about everything that's happened, I'm not sure I'm ready to share my home with Marco, or anyone else, for that matter. I need to be alone, to cry or scream if I feel like it. In fact, after yesterday's phone call saying I won't be getting a transplant, my first reaction was to crawl into a shell. It's my way of coping with unpleasant things."

Ramona sipped her tea. "Well, it's your decision. I won't say anything more about it. But would you please think it over, as a favor to me?"

"I will." She grinned. "So tell me about Marco's dancing. Do you think he's ready for a showcase?"

"He's more than ready. In fact, today we worked on the Viennese Waltz, which as you know is not an easy dance, especially for beginning students. For someone who never danced before, he's come a long way. In a month or two I might even suggest he enter a competition. There's one coming up in Scottsdale."

"I think it's an excellent idea. I can just picture him in a tuxedo. If I'm well enough, I'd like to be there to cheer him on."

Ramona stayed to chat for a few more minutes, then left and headed back to the studio.

25

When the phone rang, Marco recognized Angela's number. "Hi, Sis. I meant to call you, but I've been busy running between the restaurant and Julia's apartment."

She cut to the point. "I just spoke with Professor Rangan. He said he talked with you, but wasn't sure if it did any good. Did you even listen to what he said?"

Marco plopped down on the couch. "I respect Professor Rangan and I appreciate that he called, but I can't go back to Florida just yet. Julia's heart is getting weaker by the day. She needs me more than ever. And before you ask, the answer is no. I haven't told her about my tumor. She's depressed as it is. It didn't make any sense to add to her worries."

"Well, how long are you going to give it? The way I see it, time is running out … for both of you. There's a ticking bomb inside your head, Marco. What if something should happen to you before she gets her transplant? Have you thought about that?"

"Of course, I have. But I'm feeling fine. Believe me, the moment I feel the slightest pain, I'll be on the first flight to Miami."

A long silence, then a sigh. "I worry about you, Marco. One of the last things Mom said before she died was 'take care of Marco' and that's just what I'm trying to do."

"I know you are, and I appreciate everything you've done for me over the years. I promise I'll call more often." He didn't know what else to say as he quietly hung up.

•   •   •

Marco worked at the restaurant most of the day and part of the evening. It was a slow night and he left a couple hours early. He showed up at Julia's apartment thirty minutes later.

"Tracy was kind enough to give me a big piece of baklava." He removed it from a Styrofoam container and placed it on a paper plate. "I wasn't sure if you liked it."

"I love baklava. I haven't had it in ages. Back in Tampa, I used to go to Tarpon Springs, a Greek fishing village. They have the best Greek food in Florida. There was this one place where they made fresh baklava daily. I went there at least twice a year. I'll make us some tea, unless you prefer coffee."

"Tea is fine." They shared the baklava and afterwards reminisced about their life in Florida.

"I don't mind telling you I miss Florida," Julia said. "If it hadn't been for Ramona's invitation to come out here, I'd still be in Tampa. By the way, my aunt who lives there, called this morning and we had a long talk. She wants me to move in with her. She's a dear, sweet person, but I don't see it happening anytime soon. I wouldn't want to be a burden to her."

"Is that how you see it, being a burden? If she's serious about wanting to help, maybe you should think it over."

She nodded. "I will. I promise. Right now, my main concern is whether Dr. Levine can find another donor. He didn't sound very optimistic when I talked to him yesterday afternoon." She took a deep, labored breath. "Do you mind if I stretch out on the couch. I'm feeling a little tired."

"Of course not. I should be going, anyway." He stood to leave and grimaced as he placed his hand on the back of his head.

"Are you okay?"

He nodded. "Just a headache. I get them every once in a while. I'll take a couple of aspirins when I get back to my apartment."

She stepped closer and gave him a quick kiss and a hug. "Call me in the morning." She smiled. "Better yet, why don't you come for breakfast?"

Back in his apartment, Marco took some aspirins and waited for the headache to subside. Then he wrote in his journal.

Today, Angela asked if I had considered the possibility something could happen to me before Julia received another transplant. I told her I had thought about it, but the truth is I hadn't. I avoided the issue even though I knew my tumor could cause me to black out, or worse. The last thing I would want is to be a burden to Julia. God knows she has enough to deal with, without having to worry about me.

I'll give it some thought and come up with a plan, which I'm sure will probably involve Angela in one way or another. She is the only one I can count on. I don't know what I'd do without her. I'm blessed to have her in my life.

26

Four days later

"THERE'S SOMEONE AT THE DOOR." Marco looked at Julia from across the room. "Are you expecting anyone?"

She shook her head.

He motioned for her to remain seated. "I'll see who it is."

"I'm looking for Julia Tinsley, does she live here?" said a middle-aged woman with a somber expression. She spoke with a trace of a Native American accent.

"Yes, she does. But she's not feeling well. Can I ask—?"

"My name is Virginia Escobar. I'm Lucinda Contreras's niece. I promise I won't take too much of her time."

"That's okay," Julia said from the couch.

Marco stepped back and allowed her into the living room. She took a seat across from Marco and Julia.

"I thought you might be a friend of my aunt Lucinda and that's why I'm here. I happened to notice an unsealed envelope sitting on her nightstand. It was addressed to you. Inside was a picture taken at the San Xavier Mission. I was going to seal it and put it in the mail. But then I thought I'd come here and tell you in person."

"Tell me what?" A peculiar look filled Julia's face.

The woman cleared her throat. "She passed away in her sleep several days ago. I wasn't sure if you were a friend of hers but I thought you'd want to know."

Julia glanced at Marco. "She took our photo as we sat on a bench in one of the patios. We didn't know her, really. We only met that one time. She said her husband Alfred had passed away several months ago. She was a delightful lady and told us about her grandkids whom she didn't get to see very often."

The woman's brows furrowed. "My aunt didn't have any grandchildren. In fact she never married."

"I don't understand. Why would she make up a thing like that?" Marco said.

"I don't know what she told you, but I'll try my best to explain." The woman leaned forward. "You see, when she was young she met a young man named Alfred. That part was true. He was protestant, she was Catholic and their families didn't approve. And the fact my aunt happened to be half Mexican—half Tohono O'odham, well, it didn't make it any easier."

Julia nodded. "She said they had to run away to get married."

The woman became quiet. "I think it was all part of her fantasy, of the life she planned for herself. Actually, Alfred left to join the Army during World War II. He got killed in action somewhere in the Pacific and she never got over it."

"She was very convincing … about everything," Marco said. "She even gave us some parting advice: to cherish the moment because no one knows what the future will bring." He looked at Julia and squeezed her hand.

"It was just like her to say something like that." The woman smiled. "She loved going to the mission. That's where she and Alfred would meet at least twice a week. I learned this from her sister, my mom, who knew about their secret meetings. Their father was very strict and had ordered her to stop seeing him." She paused.

"It makes sense, when you think about it. The way she approached you and asked to take your picture. She saw you as a loving couple and it made her feel good about herself and her memories of Alfred."

"I don't know what to say. I wish we had talked to her longer," Julia said. "She didn't even give us her name. Thank you for sharing her story."

The woman stood up. "Well, I didn't mean to intrude." She pulled out the photo and handed it to Julia. "Maybe I'll see you at the mission someday. My husband and I go there for Mass whenever we happen to be in the area. I moved out of the reservation years ago, but I can't seem to stay away from San Xavier for long. There's something about it that draws me to it in a way I can't quite describe. I think my aunt felt the same way."

"I know what you mean. I've only been there twice and already I feel a part of me belongs there." Julia smiled. "Thank you for the photograph and for telling us about your aunt. Yes, maybe we'll see each other someday."

They showed the woman to the door. Then they stepped onto the balcony where a lone hummingbird appeared and sipped on water from a feeder that hung from a beam in the ceiling.

"I've never seen one close up," Marco said. "Do they come here very often?"

"Every day. That's why I have to make sure that I fill the feeder as often as I can."

She turned to Marco. "About what the woman said … that her aunt never married. She must have been very lonely. Don't you think?"

Marco shrugged. "Maybe part of what the old woman told us was true. Alfred left her with a ton of memories that sustained her throughout her entire life. If you believe in the theory of soul mates, then it's possible she led a happy life, convinced she had found and lost her soul mate. How many people go through life, looking for but never finding their one true love?"

"Do you think a person can only have one soul mate in a lifetime?"

Marco thought about it for a moment. "If you had asked me that ten years ago, I would have said yes. A person—if he's lucky—will have only one shot at finding the person he's meant to be with for eternity. But now, I'm not sure. I mean, Susan was the love of my life and I expect to see her again in another world, but …" He paused to collect his thoughts. "You are my new soul mate, Julia, regardless of why or how we met. I believe in destiny and I know I was meant to be with you at this very moment."

"I accept what you say, Marco, but a part of me still questions whether you fell in love with me only because I happen to have Susan's heart."

He stepped closer. "If you really believe me, then let's just leave it at that, okay?"

She nodded. "You're right. I think I allowed what the woman said about her aunt affect me in a way that's hard to explain. The old woman's fantasy made me wonder about us and our future together. Well, there's no point going on about it."

"No, there isn't." He smiled. "I was going to fix us a salad nicoise, but what do you say if we take a drive and stop for lunch along the way? I heard about this English tea house called Lily's, off Oracle."

"I'd like that. It'll do me good to get away from here, at least for an hour or two." She closed her eyes as Marco pressed his lips to hers. "When we get back, do you mind if we take a little nap … together. I don't know why, but I suddenly have this need to lie next to you—something we've never done before."

Marco grinned. "I'll look forward to it. Let's get out of here."

27

MARCO SAT AT A TABLE toward the back of the bar, waiting for Max to appear. His unexpected phone call had left him wondering what he was up to and why he'd chosen to meet at the Mad Coyote, a biker hangout. He drank his beer and looked at his watch. Max was late. He'd give him another ten minutes and then … he spotted him as he came through the door. Max wore a blue T-shirt over a pair of tan cargo pants and nodded as he made his way to Marco's table.

"Thanks for meeting me." Max took a seat. He signaled to one of the waitresses. "Ever been here before?"

Marco shook his head.

"Well, as you can see, it's mostly bikers who come here. I have a Harley and ride it on weekends. See that guy in the corner with a red bandana?" He pointed. "He's an orthopedic surgeon. The two tough-looking guys at the table next to him are retired schoolteachers."

The waitress appeared and took Max's order for a Tecate with extra limes. He continued. "Bikers tend to get a bad rap, but as you can see, we come from all walks of life."

"So what is it you want to tell me?" Marco said, an impatient tone to his voice.

Max crossed his arms and leaned back in his chair. "Let's get one thing straight. I don't like you, and maybe the feeling is mutual."

"If that's what you had to say, you could have done that on the phone. Look, I know you think I stole your girl, but—"

"Forget it, that's not why I asked you to meet me." He paused to allow the waitress to deliver the beer. "I wanted to talk to you about … how can I say this without sounding like I'm still trying to win her back?" He took a gulp of his beer. "I'll cut to the chase. I've known Julia for almost three years. She's a very fragile woman in more ways than one. And even though we broke up, I still care about her and want her to be happy. More than that, I want her to be safe and secure in what may be the last days of her life."

"What are you talking about?"

Max took another gulp. "I'm talking about the real possibility that she may not get another transplant. That's why I wanted to talk to you, to make sure you're not going to bail out on her." He stared at him for a second. "She's going to get a lot sicker, you know that don't you?"

"Of course I do," Marco snapped. "And I don't need you to question what I will or won't do. But since you brought it up, I would never leave her. Not now, not ever. She means the world to me."

"I'm glad to hear that, because …" Max softened his tone. "I'm a personal trainer and I've just been offered a position in Denver. I didn't want to accept it until I had a chance to talk to you. And now that I have, I feel a lot better, knowing that Julia won't be alone in the days to come." He smiled. "Maybe I misjudged you. You seem like a stand-up guy. Sorry we got off on the wrong foot." He lifted his bottle. "This calls for a toast. To Julia."

Marco did the same. "To Julia," he echoed.

"Did Julia ever tell you how we met?" Max said, sounding more relaxed.

"Not that I recall."

"Well, one night as I left the supermarket near the dance studio, I heard a woman call for help at the other end of the parking lot. I rushed over and saw a man trying to steal her purse. He took off toward the street. I wanted to chase after him and beat the crap out of him, but I stayed back to help her. Anyway, that's how we met. The next day I asked her out for a cup of coffee. We started dating from that point on. Looking back, I know that maybe we weren't the best match. I hate dancing and she hates motorcycles." He shrugged. "It was an opposites-attract kind of thing."

"Are you going to tell her … about your new job in Denver?"

"I think I should. But don't worry, I won't mention that we had this little meeting." Max hesitated. "Can you do me a favor?" He wrote his phone number on a piece of paper and handed it to him. "Call me if …" He paused as though unable to finish his thought.

Marco nodded. "I understand."

"Well, I have to run—got a lot of things to take care of if I expect to leave by the end of the week." He got up and dropped a ten-dollar bill on the table. "Thanks again for hearing me out."

Marco stayed back to finish his beer. He didn't quite know what to make of Max or his feelings for Julia. In a way he admired him for wanting to make sure she'd have someone to look after her. He wished they had talked longer. But under the circumstances, it was just as well that they didn't.

•   •   •

Marco worked at the restaurant the rest of the day. He talked to Julia during his break and later in the evening. He promised to see her in the morning.

Before retiring, he wrote in his journal:

Today I met with Max, Julia's ex-boyfriend. We talked about Julia and her uncertain future. He was more pessimistic than me about her chances of getting another transplant. From the beginning it was clear we had little in common, except for our love for Julia, and it made me wonder: would they have gotten back together if she hadn't suffered a miscarriage? It was a topic that Julia had yet to bring up. Whatever the answer, I could tell that Max was a solid kind of guy who had been her protector as much as her friend and lover. He had come into her life when she needed someone to lean on.

Perhaps the saying is true: people come into our lives for a reason, a season or a lifetime. Max was clearly a season, which means that I am here for either a reason or a lifetime. Only time will tell.

28

MARCO WENT PALE seeing an emergency vehicle in front of Julia's apartment. *God, please let her be okay*, he prayed as he pulled into the lot.

Julia sat on the curb surrounded by paramedics and a couple of neighbors. He rushed toward her. "Are you all right?"

"I feel fine." She held her head with her hands. "I must have blacked out or something."

"We got a call about a woman who had collapsed on the sidewalk," said one of the paramedics. "When we got here, we found her in a semi-conscious state. Are you her husband?"

"I'm a friend. Is she going to be okay?"

"She's fine now, but she should be seen by a doctor just to make sure. She didn't want us to take her to the hospital. Will you stay with her?"

Marco nodded. "I'll make sure she gets some rest." He took her hand and walked her up to the apartment.

"I think the paramedic was right, about seeing a doctor." Marco eased her onto the couch. He removed her sandals and sat next to her.

"I'm fine, really. To tell you the truth I feel a little embarrassed. People gawking at me and paramedics wanting to take me to the hospital." She attempted a smile. "I'm glad you showed up when you did."

"So what happened?"

She sighed, then ran her fingers through her hair. "I was on the balcony and saw people walking across the lawn. They seemed to have not a care in the world. I envied them. The next moment, I put on my sandals and went for a stroll. It was an impulse kind of thing. I meant to walk for a few minutes, just up to the next building and back. But the day was so beautiful I walked longer than I should have. I fainted as I neared my apartment."

"You gave me quite a scare, I want you to know. Please promise me that you won't do that again. I mean, taking such a long walk alone."

"You're beginning to sound like Max. Look, Marco, I have to be free to do what I want, even if it means taking risks." She shook her head. "You just don't know what it's like, being cooped up in this place day after day."

Marco put his arm around her and looked into her eyes. "I worry about you and I don't want to lose you." He kissed her and softened his tone. "Take all the walks that you want but keep your cell phone handy. Okay?"

She nodded. "By the way, Max called a couple hours ago. He's leaving town and he wanted to say goodbye. After I wished him well, he said something that surprised me a little. He said I was lucky to have you in my life."

"It was nice of him to say that," Marco said after a pause. He wondered what else Max had told her. Not that it mattered. He would soon be out of town and out of her life.

"Let's go out on the balcony." She smiled. "I want to say hi to my little friends."

"Your little friends?" They got up and stepped onto the balcony, where a sudden gust of wind caused the bamboo wind chimes to clatter.

A minute later a hummingbird appeared. It took a quick sip of water and flew away. "That's Pierre," she said, smiling. "He shows up about this time, every day."

"Pierre? You named him Pierre? Odd name for a hummingbird." He chuckled. "How can you tell one hummingbird from another?"

"Oh, I can tell. Pierre is unique. Believe me, I know my hummingbirds. Louise and Elsie come later in the afternoon." She said it with a straight face.

Marco stifled a laugh. "Well, I'm happy that you've gotten to know them so well."

Julia smiled, but only for a second. "There's something you should know." She hesitated. "About Max and I. We actually talked for several minutes and it brought back a lot memories, some of which I've tried to block out, unsuccessfully, I might add."

"You really don't have to do this. As far as I'm concerned what happened between you and Max is your business. Besides, it's all in the past."

"I appreciate you saying that, but now that he's completely out of my life, I feel you should know more about me." She paused. "Let's go inside."

They sat on the couch. Julia continued. "The day I collapsed at the studio, I was two months pregnant. When I awoke in the hospital I found out I had miscarried. Max saw it as a blessing in disguise. Of course, I was devastated. I wanted to have the baby even though Max was against it. He thought I was too fragile due to my transplant. We argued about it many times, as you can imagine."

Marco nodded. "It makes sense now … the day you showed up late for my lesson."

"Max had always been good to me, but he was overly protective, to the point that I felt smothered, especially the past few months. I wanted to be myself. To be free to do what felt natural, like I did before I had the transplant." She let out a sigh. "I know he meant well and he did care about me during our time together."

"Do you mind if I ask you a question?" Brief pause. "What would have happened if you had given birth to the baby?"

"What do you mean?"

"Would you have gone back to Max? Would you have considered marrying him?"

She thought about it for a moment. "I don't know how to answer that because we never really had any serious talks about it. Max had been married twice and he feared being a three-time loser—his words not mine. We basically took it one day at a time, which was okay with me considering I was still trying to make sense of my own failed marriage. To be honest, I think he would have made a great dad."

Ramona had told him about her pregnancy, but it was good to hear it from Julia. She had shared a deeply personal experience, and it made him love her all the more. He smiled a little. "You didn't have to tell me anything, but I'm glad you did. I used to think that some things should stay in the past where they belong. Now, I'm not so sure."

A mischievous smile crossed her face. "So, are there any dark secrets from your past? Something you've never shared with anyone?"

For a second, he considered telling her about his tumor, but held back knowing it was neither the time nor the place to mention it. Her reaction would've ruined the closeness of the moment. "I really can't think of any. But there is something that has haunted me for many years." He hesitated. "When I was in high school I had a girlfriend—my first love, you might say. We got along great and we both assumed we'd go on to college together. Then, right before graduation, I broke it off and we went our separate ways. Over the years, I thought about her … about the night she gave herself to me. She looked at it as a commitment to our relationship, something that would bind us together for the rest of our lives." He paused for a moment. "I took a precious thing from her and I've been punishing myself for it ever since."

"You shouldn't be so hard on yourself. You were young and inexperienced, about life and especially about love." She placed her hand over his.

"You're right." Marco nodded, then continued. "Let me tell you the rest. About six years ago, I decided to look her up, to see how she was doing. Actually, a part of me wanted to make things right, if it were possible. I hoped she'd be available. I had heard she was a schoolteacher and so I drove to the school where she taught the third grade. I had no real plan as I sat in my car in front of the building. At first I thought about going inside and surprising her. But then I realized the shock of seeing me after all these years would be too much for her. So, I drove away from the school. About a week later I checked her name through the internet." He shook his head. "I couldn't believe it. I was in shock for the rest of the day."

"What did you find?"

"Her obituary. She had moved to California where she died giving birth to her second child." He released a long sigh. "Of all the things I expected to find, her death notice wasn't one of them. For a second I wished I hadn't tried to find her. It would have been easier for me, to keep her memory in the recesses of my mind, a far safer place than reality."

"Marco, you have to let go of it—the guilt or whatever you're feeling—because if you don't, it will eat away at your soul."

"I know." He closed his eyes for a moment. "I liken my memory of her to a box that you store away on a shelf and every once in a while it falls to the floor. You pick it up, examine it and put it back on the shelf. It's been a long time since the box fell to the floor. Anyway, it was something I wanted to share with you … something I've never told anyone else."

"Thanks for sharing that with me, even though you really didn't have to." She paused. "I feel really tired. Do you mind if I take a short nap?" She paused again. "You can join me if you like."

"That's the best offer I've had all day." He smiled as he followed her to the bedroom.

29

T HE PHONE RANG just before 9:00 a.m. Marco hesitated before answering it.

"I'm calling for Dr. Goldstein," said a woman who sounded as though she was just getting over a cold. "He's concerned because you failed to set a new date for your surgery. He wanted me to provide you with the name of a doctor in Tucson who is prepared to take over your case."

"I had meant to call him but I've been extremely busy. Can you please tell him that—?"

"Do you have a pen and paper handy?"

Marco looked around and grabbed a paper napkin from the kitchen counter. "Go ahead." He listened as she gave him the surgeon's name and phone number. "Thank you," he said and hung up.

He hadn't expected to hear from Dr. Goldstein and wondered if his sister had talked to him. If she had, the referral to a local physician made sense. He had no excuse now for not seeing a doctor and it would be hard to explain why he hadn't made an appointment. He slipped the napkin in his back pocket. On his way to work, he dropped by Julia's apartment. He couldn't stay long and promised to call before the end of the night.

Later, during a break, he returned a call from Ramona.

She had something that she wanted to discuss with him. "Are you free tomorrow night?" she asked.

"I think so. At least I'm not scheduled to work."

"Well, here's what we're planning …" She filled him on the details for a surprise party for Julia. "We want to let her know that we miss her and we're behind her one hundred percent. Everybody will be there … her students, other teachers and even the lady who sews the gowns."

"So, what do you want me to do?"

"Tell Julia you want to take her out to dinner or some other place. When you pass the studio, say that you need to drop by to pick up a new pair of shoes that you ordered. Bring her inside and we'll do the rest."

"The rest?"

"That's all I can tell you for now. Can you do it? Can you make sure she'll be here at seven o'clock?"

Marco hesitated. "Okay, one way or another I'll get her to the studio."

Before going to bed, Marco wrote about it in his journal.

I'm having second thoughts about taking Julia to the studio the way Ramona had suggested. Though I'm sure she'd love to see her friends and students, a long evening might be too much for her. I'll sleep on it and make up my mind in the morning.

A moment later, he wrote:

All day, I've been thinking about the phone call from Dr. Goldstein's office. I know I should make an appointment with the local doctor as soon possible. But I don't know if I'm ready. I'm actually afraid. What if something should go wrong during the surgery? Who would take care of Julia? I pray for a miracle … for both of us.

30

"WHAT'S ALL THE MYSTERY ABOUT?" Julia said as she got into Marco's car. "Where are you taking me?"

Marco smiled. "You'll see."

Minutes later he pulled into the lot in front of the Sonoran Ballroom. It looked closed. No lights, no people, nothing to indicate that dancers might soon be arriving.

She looked puzzled. "I don't understand. What are we doing here?"

Marco didn't respond. He got out and came around to open her door. "Let's go inside. I need to pick up a pair of shoes that I ordered. They walked up to the entrance.

"But it's closed, Marco."

Marco pulled on the door. "No, it isn't." He held it open and she stepped into the studio.

Suddenly the lights came on, and people came out from behind the counter and the backrooms. "Surprise! Surprise!" they shouted.

Julia covered her mouth. "Oh my God. What are you all doing here?"

Ramona stepped forward. "We want to show our support in the only way we know how—by putting on a special dance in your honor." She reached to give her a big hug. "We love you and we miss you."

Julia started to cry. She turned to Marco. "You knew about this, and you didn't say anything."

Marco grinned. "It was supposed to be a surprise."

Everyone waited for Marco and Julia to dance the first selection, a slow waltz from the movie, *The Godfather.*

Marco extended his hand. "May I have this dance?"

Dressed in a long, dark blue dress, Julia took his hand and got into frame.

Then they took the first steps, slowly making their way around the room, past smiling students, teachers, and guests. When it was over, everyone clapped and joined them on the floor, ready to dance the next selection: *Black Magic Woman,* a *cha-cha* by the Carlos Santana band.

"I think I'll sit this one out," Julia said, slightly out of breath. She held her hand to her chest.

Marco expected her to say that. They took a seat at a table next to a mirrored wall above which hung portraits of famous dancers, from Gene Kelly to Fred Astaire and even some celebrities from the TV show, *Dancing with the Stars.*

Later, two of Julia's students took to the floor. They danced a tango they had choreographed especially for her. She smiled and tapped her feet to the staccato-like sounds of the music. Ever the teacher, she nodded approvingly as they executed one pattern after another: the fan, the promenade, the corté, and even some stylized turns. Like most tangos, it ended with a dramatic flair.

"Bravo! Bravo! Well done," Julia shouted, while everyone clapped.

Julia enjoyed the evening, surrounded by former students and well-wishers. Most took a moment to chat with her and Marco. Some took photographs and promised to stay in touch.

Toward the end of the hour and a half dance, Ramona stopped the music and passed out empty goblets. At the same time, Alan, the owner of the studio, opened a bottle of champagne. He poured a little into each glass. Then Ramona lifted hers and waited for everyone to do the same. "To Julia. A great friend and a great teacher. We love you always."

"To Julia," everyone echoed.

After a moment, Ramona put down her glass and turned to Julia. "The last dance belongs to you and Marco." She signaled to one of the teachers to play another waltz.

Smiling, Marco stood up and extended his hand.

Julia seemed overwhelmed. Tears trickled down her face as she got up and took Marco's hand. While everyone watched, they danced, from one end of the room to the other. When the piece ended, Marco and Julia stayed in frame, long enough for Marco to kiss her on the lips. She blushed as everyone clapped and cheered.

They left shortly afterward and drove back to Julia's apartment.

A perfect ending to a perfect night, Marco mused as he tucked her into bed. Exhausted, she fell asleep the moment her head hit the pillow.

Marco smiled as he wrote in his journal, just before going to bed.

Thanks to Ramona, Julia had a chance to be with her students, fellow teachers, and well-wishers. Initially I feared a long night would be too much for her. I had considered telling Ramona that Julia wouldn't be able to make it. But I'm glad I didn't. It was exactly what Julia needed. Dancing was her life and for almost two hours, it lifted her spirits, and mine as well. For a moment I almost forgot she was sick. More likely I just wanted to block it out of my mind, if only temporarily. Regardless, it gave us the opportunity to reveal to everyone, that she and I are in love. I'm smiling, still, as I relive the moment I kissed her and held her in my arms, long after the waltz had stopped playing. That alone, made it all worthwhile.

31

M ARCO SHOWED UP at the studio a little before 10:00 a.m. Ramona greeted him with a hug and took a moment to talk, mostly about Julia. "I hope it wasn't too much for her, the dancing and all the excitement."

"Maybe a little, but it was well worth it. She hadn't seen many of her students in a long time. And when Art and Margaret danced the Tango, well, she couldn't have been more pleased."

"How is she doing?"

"As good as can be expected. As for a new transplant, well ..." He shrugged. "It's anybody's guess when it might happen. She has an appointment with her doctor tomorrow morning and maybe we'll have some good news."

Ramona became quiet. "If something were to happen, I mean if she doesn't get a transplant in time and she needs someone to ..." She paused as though to search for the right words. "What I'm trying to say is I want to be there for her, even if you have to call at two o'clock in the morning."

"I understand." He nodded. "You're not the first person who's asked to be notified." He sighed. "I pray that it won't be necessary."

"Well, whatever happens I want you to know I'll be there for you as well." She smiled. "Let's begin your lesson. I thought we might try something new. The bolero. It's not for beginning students, but I think you can handle it. We might even add a few extra patterns if you decide to do a showcase. Julia and I think you're ready, so maybe we'll work on preparing something special. Then when you feel more comfortable, we'll see about entering you in a competition."

Marco frowned, slightly. Spending additional hours practicing for a competition would mean less time with Julia. More than ever, he valued his time with her and he wished Ramona hadn't mentioned it.

•   •   •

Later, Marco picked up a few grocery items and dropped them off at Julia's apartment. He didn't stay long—he had to run over to the restaurant to cover for one of the cooks who failed to show. Throughout the drive he couldn't get the phone call from Dr. Goldstein's office out of his mind. He dreaded having to meet a new doctor. As he neared the restaurant, it occurred to him that maybe the new doctor would have a different opinion. Maybe he would allow him to put off the surgery for a month or two. He parked behind the restaurant and gave himself a moment. Then he called Dr. Molinar's office.

They had been expecting his call and set up an appointment the day after tomorrow. He closed his eyes for a second and prayed he'd made the right decision.

"You seem distracted," Tracy said during a mid-afternoon break.

"That's because I am." He frowned, slightly. "I've got a lot on my mind and I wish I knew what to do."

"Well, whatever is happening in your life, I hope you know you can count on me, for advice or whatever." She smiled. "I'm a little older than you and I've had my share of life's tribulations. Anyway, if there's any way I can help …"

"Can I confide in you about something?" He paused for a moment. "It's about my girlfriend Julia who has a bad heart. I never talked about her much, but she's sick, very sick, and I'm really worried about her. She needs a transplant. The trouble is she already had one, which means her chances of getting another are pretty slim."

"Oh, Marco, I'm so sorry. I can imagine what you must be going through. Is there no hope, whatsoever? I mean, they can't just give up on her."

A deep sigh. "There's always hope, but she may not last long enough to receive a new heart. She's supposed to see the doctor tomorrow and we're praying he'll have some encouraging news."

"Well, whatever happens, I want you to know I'm in your corner. Now that I know your situation, I'll try not to bug you so often." She grinned.

Marco shook his head. "I need the money. So please, continue to call whenever you need me. Besides, when I'm here I'm forced to think about something else. The truth is, if I didn't work I'd probably hang around Julia's apartment. Not good for either one us. She needs her space and I need my own time to think and plan for the future. Of course, if she should take a turn for the worse …" He stared away for a second. "I don't even want to think about it."

"Well, like I said, if there's anything I can do, I'll be more than happy to help."

Marco thought about it. He'd been less than candid about the reason for his distracted demeanor, which had as much to do with Julia as with his decision to see a doctor. So far, he'd not told anyone. He needed someone to confide in, to reassure him, like his sister would, that everything would be okay. He hesitated. "There's something else that I want to tell you, not about Julia but about me."

A quizzical look crossed Tracy's face.

"The thing is, I'm supposed to see a doctor, the day after tomorrow. It's something I've been putting off for a long time, mostly because of Julia. I worried that if something happened to me, she—"

One of the servers interrupted. "You have a phone call, Tracy. A guy from Green Valley wanting to know if you can cater a wedding in two weeks."

Tracy turned to Marco. "Sorry, Marco, but I've got to take this call."

Marco nodded. In a way he felt relieved he didn't finish telling her about his tumor. She would've asked too many questions, for which he'd have few good answers. Besides, the last thing he needed was another "big" sister, nagging at him half the time.

32

J ULIA DIDN'T HAVE TO SAY ANYTHING—her face said it all—as she came through the doorway and joined Marco in the waiting room. When she finally spoke, she seemed almost resigned, as though she knew her fate had already been decided by forces beyond the control of mere mortals. "The doctor thinks I should get my affairs in order."

"Wh-what happened?"

"Let's get out of here, I'll explain later."

They left the office and strode back to the car. "I don't feel like going back to my apartment." She turned to Marco. "There's a park called Agua Caliente a few miles out of town. I used to go there whenever I felt a little down or I needed to see some water and tall palm trees like they have in Florida. Let's go there. Do you mind?"

"Not at all. I've never been there." He followed her directions: east on Tanque Verde for several miles, then north on a narrow road that cut through the desert. When he spotted a sign that said Agua Caliente, he slowed and turned into yet another road. Just ahead, an oasis of huge palm trees and small ponds.

They pulled into the visitor's lot, got out and began to stroll. "It feels like we're in the everglades, or pretty close to it," Marco said. A sudden gust of wind whirled above them, causing a large palm frond to fall to the ground. They walked around it and made their way to the water's edge, where wild ducks played and made quacking sounds that attracted a little boy and a girl.

"Let's sit down," Julia said. They ambled up to a picnic table.

Her mind seemed to be miles away as she closed her eyes and then opened them again. "I don't know where to begin. When the doctor hinted that I should consider putting my affairs in order, I was stunned. He had never talked that way before, so I naturally assumed the worst." She let out a sigh. "He told me that a couple of days ago, I had a good chance of getting a woman's heart. But when her family found out I had received a previous heart they insisted it go to a first time recipient. It went to a forty-two-year-old woman."

"He's not giving up on you, is he?"

She shook her head. "But he did say that my heart is weaker than it was a few weeks ago and if I don't receive a new heart soon, well …"

"You can't give up, Julia. I believe in miracles and I know something good is going to come your way. I can feel it, almost like a premonition." He reached to hold her hand. "We're in this together. I mean it."

She hesitated. "I'm glad you said that because I've done a lot of thinking. Not just because of what happened today, though I have to admit it made me realize that I can't afford to wait any longer." A long pause. "I-I've got to make arrangements for myself."

"You don't mean …?"

She nodded. "As much as I hate to think about it, I've got to at least make some inquires. Will you help me?"

"I … don't know what to say. Yes, of course I'll help you." He gave himself a moment, his mind shutting out the implications of her question. "Why don't we talk about it some other time? Let's pretend we're here just to enjoy the park." He smiled. "Too bad we didn't bring a picnic basket."

"I'm sorry. I really didn't mean to get heavy about this. I had meant to discuss it with you before, but I couldn't bring myself to talk about it."

"I understand." He stood up. "It's such a beautiful day. Let's walk around." As they strolled back to the water's edge, they saw the same little boy and girl throwing pieces of bread to the ducks in the water. When the little boy spotted a small turtle heading toward a patch of wet grass near a wooden bridge, he ran over and picked it up. His mother yelled at him to put it down. The boy reluctantly set it down and went back to feeding the ducks.

Marco and Julia continued to walk through the park. After almost an hour, they drove to Julia's apartment. Too tired to do anything else, Julia went straight to bed and took a nap. Marco lay beside her.

Later, Marco returned to his apartment. He stayed up till midnight and wrote in his journal.

Today, Julia surprised me when she asked if I would help her make funeral arrangements. I tried to stay calm, though inside I trembled with fear because it meant the end was nearer than I had anticipated. She's taking it well, a lot better than I would, and I have to give her credit for that. She's a survivor and she's proved it once again. Sometimes I wish we were a normal couple with ordinary problems. Tomorrow is my turn to face the doctor and I'm tempted to cancel the appointment. Except for an occasional headache, I feel fine. Maybe I can put off the operation indefinitely. Just one more month is all I pray for.

33

MARCO SAT IN DR. MOLINAR'S OFFICE, waiting to be called. Restless, he got up and wandered over to a quiet corner and dialed Julia's number. No answer. He tried again ten minutes later. Still no answer. Maybe she was in the shower or in the bedroom taking a nap.

"Mr. Anissi?" said a young woman who emerged from one of the rooms. She wore pink scrubs and held a black clipboard with a pen attached to a long chain.

Marco nodded and followed her through a set of doors that led to one of the patients' rooms. "Please have seat. Dr. Molinar will be with you shortly."

Marco sat in a chair facing a chart of the brain, similar to the one in Dr. Goldstein's office in Miami. He averted his eyes from it and looked around for something to read. A couple of magazines caught his eye: *The New Yorker* and *Ladies Home Journal.* He picked up *The New Yorker* and thumbed through it.

Five minutes later, the woman in the pink scrubs appeared. "Dr. Molinar is running late. You're next on his list, though."

She smiled. "Shouldn't be no more than ten or twelve minutes."

"No problem. I'm not in a hurry." Marco went back to *The New Yorker*. After reading a couple of articles, he put down the magazine and glanced at his watch.

His phone rang. "I'm worried about Julia," said Ramona. "I called her twice within the past twenty minutes and got no answer."

"I've been trying to reach her myself. Look, do me a favor. If she should call, can you please let me know?" He hung up the phone and dialed Julia's number. It was still ringing when he got up and hurried out the door.

Back in his car, he tried again. Still no answer. He sped all the way to her apartment and got there twenty minutes later.

He knocked on her door, waited a moment and knocked again. No response. He pulled out a key that Julia had given him and let himself in. "Julia, are you okay?" He rushed to the bedroom. She lay face down on the bed. An open bottle of pills sat on the nightstand. "Oh, no. Julia, Julia. Wake up, wake up." He shook her and turned her over. When she opened her eyes, he let out a sigh. "Talk to me, Julia. Say something, anything."

Julia stared at Marco as though she didn't understand why he hovered over her.

"How do you feel?" He picked up her hand and squeezed it.

"What … what are you doing here?" She seemed dazed and confused.

"I tried calling, but you didn't answer, so I came over to see if you were okay."

"I couldn't sleep and I took a sleeping pill." She sat up. "What time is it?

"It's ten-thirty in the morning." He gave her a couple of seconds, then helped her out of bed. "Let's go into the living room."

They sat on the couch. "I'm sorry you had to come here and see me like this." She yawned as she took a deep breath. "I didn't mean to worry you."

"I think you could use some coffee." He stood up, walked over to the kitchen and put on a pot. A moment later he poured a cup and brought it to her. "I made it a little strong."

She took a quick sip and set it down. "I feel embarrassed. I hate losing control. I probably would have been better off if I drank a glass of wine instead."

"How many pills did you take?"

"I know what you're thinking." She reached for her cup. "I took one pill and couldn't go to sleep, so I took another." She attempted a smile. "I'm not ready to throw in the towel, just yet." She brushed her hair with her hand. "I must look like a mess. Can you give me a few minutes? I want to take a shower and change into something comfortable."

"While you're doing that, I'll make you some breakfast." He paused, then called Ramona. He got her voice mail and left a message.

Marco could hear the shower running as he beat some eggs for an omelet. When his phone rang, he waited a second before answering it. "Yes." He nodded. "I know I should have told someone, but something came up and I had to leave quickly. All I can say is I'm sorry."

"We'll have to charge for a missed appointment and schedule you for another day. Unfortunately, the earliest Dr. Molinar could see you would be toward the end of next week. He has an opening on Thursday at two in the afternoon."

Marco thought about it. "Let me check my calendar. I'll call you back later." As he hung up he spotted a brochure on the floor next to the table: MOST FREQUENTLY ASKED QUESTIONS ABOUT HOSPICE. He picked it up and set it down on the counter. Then he went back to the omelet.

"Hmm … smells good." Julia sounded cheerful and alert. Her hair tied back with a small barrette, she wore a red Mexican dress that came down to her slippers. She sat at the table, which had a single setting and a fresh cup of coffee.

"I found a couple of strips of bacon and a green pepper and put them together, along with some spinach that looked a bit wilted. Hope you like it." He placed it in front of her and sat down beside her.

Julia smiled as she tasted the omelet. "I love it. I hope you'll make it again."

"I will, only next time I'll add some cheese, which you didn't have in your refrigerator." They talked while she ate. When she finished, she moved the plate to the side and sipped on her coffee.

"By the way, I saw a brochure on the floor, about hospice. Don't you think it's a bit soon to be thinking about—?"

"It came in the mail yesterday morning and I didn't open it until a few minutes before going to bed. To be honest, I don't know why they sent it to me. It depressed me to the point that I couldn't sleep. That's why I took the pills."

"Who could have sent it to you?"

She shrugged. "Probably my doctor or someone in his office. It's like they're all giving up on me." She sighed. "I wish I hadn't read it. When I went to bed and took the second pill I thought how easy it would be to take more pills just to fall asleep and never wake up. I almost called you but I figured you were already asleep."

Marco reached across and held her hand. "Listen to me. If you ever have those thoughts again, I want you to call me. No matter the time. I mean it. You don't have to go it alone. Do you understand?"

Julia nodded. "I'm so glad you came into my life. I just wish it had been under different circumstances." She brushed away a tear from the side of her face.

"Hey, don't get too heavy on me." He smiled. "Want to see what Ramona taught me during our last lesson?"

"Sure." She flashed a quick smile.

Marco stood up and held his arms around an imaginary partner. "I won't tell you what I'm dancing. Let's see if you can figure it out." He took a few long steps and made broad movements with his hands and arms on almost every beat. He did this for a couple minutes as he danced around the room and came to a stop inches away from Julia. "Well, can you name the dance?"

Julia took a moment to answer. "The bolero. You did very well. I'll have to tell Ramona she's doing an excellent job. Though I'm a little jealous."

Marco remained standing as he extended his hand. "Let's dance. Just for a minute. We'll take it slow and easy."

Julia hesitated, then stood up and got into frame. They smiled as they danced the bolero, without music and without having to worry about missing a step. When they stopped, Marco moved closer and gave her a long, tender kiss. They were in a tight embrace when the phone rang, and she broke away to answer it.

"I'm fine, Ramona. Marco is here with me. We're in the middle of practicing the bolero steps that you taught him." She nodded. "I'll call you later and tell you all about it." More nodding, then she hung up. "Where were we?" She grinned.

34

Three days later

WHEN THE PHONE RANG, Marco waited a moment before answering it. "Hi, Sis. Things have been pretty hectic around here. That's why I haven't—"

"Did someone from Dr. Goldstein's office call you about seeing a doctor in Tucson?"

"They did. His secretary gave me the name of a local doctor. I made an appointment and went to his office, but ..." He paused. "You may as well know the truth. I didn't get to see him."

"Let me guess. It had something to do with Julia. Oh, Marco." She let out a sigh. "So, what are you going to do?"

"I don't know. Right now I can only think about Julia. Her doctor practically told her to get her affairs in order, so it's no longer about when or if she'll get a new heart. She knows the end is near and I want to be there for her. I love her, Sis. I can't bail out on her, not even for a day."

Angela was silent for a long while. "You haven't told her, have you?"

Marco took a moment. "I didn't want to add to her worries. She's depressed as it is. Besides, I'm feeling fine. In fact, I haven't had a headache in days."

"You're having headaches? You never told me that."

"Well, just mild ones. Trust me. If I ever got a really bad one, I'd go straight to the emergency."

"I'm glad you said that," she said, relief in her voice. "But I'll feel a lot better when you make another appointment with the doctor. You are going to make another appointment, aren't you?"

"I won't lie to you. I'm not going to do anything until I know what's happening with Julia."

"Okay, Marco have it your way," she said in a yielding tone. "But please, please stay in touch. Call me and let me know what's going on. No matter what happens, I'm here for you. I hope you know that."

"Thanks, Sis. There's no one else I'd rather have by my side than you." He hung up with a lump in his throat, then dialed Julia's number. He needed to hear her voice, if only for a minute. Her voice mail answered. "Hi Julia," he said unable to hide his disappointment. "I'm running late and I have to be at the restaurant in half an hour. I'll call you during my break. Love you."

Marco worked the entire day and spoke to Julia during his break and later as he got ready to leave. "I know it's late, but I can drop by for a few minutes, to tuck you in. I'll even bring a piece of baklava that you like so much. What do you say?"

"Thanks, but I'm already in bed. Can you come over tomorrow for a late breakfast? I need to discuss something with you." She was silent for a moment. "It's better if I tell you in person."

"It sounds serious. Can you give me a hint?"

"Well, I've given the matter a lot of thought, about making final arrangements. It was unfair of me to ask you to help me. Can we table the whole subject, at least until … God, it's so hard for me to even talk about it."

"Of course, I'll do whatever you say."

She sighed. "This morning I sat down and wrote a set of instructions which will explain everything, especially my wishes about … about the funeral. I put everything in an envelope. I'll leave it on top of the coffee table."

The idea that she had written final instructions left him momentarily speechless. "Well, I know it's late and you need to go to bed," he finally said. "I'll see you around nine." He got in his car and headed back to his apartment.

Minutes later, his phone rang and he answered on the first ring. He hoped it'd be Julia. It was her ex-boyfriend, Max.

"I had to come back for a couple of days to take care of some business and I thought I'd give you a call. How is Julia?"

"She's doing okay. I mean, as good as can be expected." He pulled to the side of the road. "I'll give it to you straight. She won't be getting a new transplant. Her heart may give out on her at any moment. Her doctor has pretty much given up on her, which I can't really understand. I was going to tell you about it, so it's just as well that you called."

"I wish there was something I could do. Yesterday I drove to her complex for no special reason. Later, I thought about calling her, just to say hello."

"I don't think it would be a good idea. She's playing this thing close to the chest and few people know she may not last more than a few weeks."

Max was silent. "I'm going to say something to you, something I never said to Julia." He paused. "I love her very much. Maybe if I had told her that months ago, we'd still be together." His voice started to break. "Take care of her. I'll leave it up to you to call me when you think …" He hung up as though unable to finish the sentence.

Marco waited a moment before getting back on the road. For a second he almost felt sorry for Max. He believed him when he said he loved her. If he had said those words to her would it have made a difference? He wondered. But it was late and he didn't want to dwell on it, not when he had bigger things on his mind.

35

M ARCO SHOWED UP at Julia's apartment just before 9:00 a.m. He wrapped his arms around her and held her tightly as though he hadn't seen her in a long time. "I love you," he said, allowing the moment to linger.

"I love you, too. What a wonderful way to start the day."

She stepped into the kitchen. "I hope you're hungry. I felt pretty good this morning, so I decided to make pancakes and some extra crispy bacon to go with them."

Marco took a whiff and smiled. "There's nothing like the smell of cooked bacon, especially in the morning. Let me help you."

"No. You just sit down and I'll do everything. I like cooking and serving you for a change."

Marco took a seat and waited for Julia to bring the pancakes to the table.

"Help yourself." She sat across from him. They ate while they talked, and when they were finished, got up and moved to the couch.

Julia's good mood faded. "The instructions I told you about are inside *The Prophet,* right there on the coffee table. I thought about showing them to you, but it's probably best if you wait until …" She stopped herself, as though afraid to finish the thought. "Anyway, that's where I put them. By the way, you're the only one who knows they exist."

Marco stared at the book but didn't say anything. He wished she hadn't mentioned it. Bad enough he had to put on a false face to conceal the anguish he felt every time he saw her, every time he kissed her and held her in his arms.

"Yesterday, I went out for a walk and when I returned to my apartment I saw a silver Honda that looked like Max's car leaving the complex. It made me wonder about him. You don't suppose he's back in town, do you?"

Marco shrugged. "Listen, I have to check on a book I ordered at a bookstore on Speedway. Want to come along? On the way back we can pick up a video. But I can't stay past three o'clock. Tracy wanted me to come in early for a special dinner to raise money for a homeless shelter."

Julia smiled. "It'll do me good to get some fresh air. Just give me a moment while I touch up my face and change into something more presentable."

"You look fine to me." He grinned. "Take as much time as you need."

•   •   •

When they walked into the store, he spotted the book on the counter: *A Dozen Invisible Pieces and Other Confessions of Motherhood.*

Julia chuckled when she saw the cover showing a pregnant woman. "You're buying a book about motherhood?"

"I met the author at a writer's conference and she told me about her book. It's a memoir. I had been meaning to buy it for a long time and a few days ago I went ahead and ordered it." He paid for the book and stepped away.

"Can I read it after you finish?" She thumbed through the pages, then looked at the back cover which had a picture of the author, Kimmelin Hull, and a brief summary.

"Sure. You can read it first, if you want."

They had neared the door when the sales lady called out to him. "I forgot to tell you, the medical book you ordered, the one about the brain is still on back order. We expect to receive it sometime this week."

Marco cleared his throat. "I changed my mind. I don't need it," he said curtly. He turned to Julia. "I started to write a short story about … about a guy who undergoes brain surgery, and I wanted to read up on the subject. But I didn't like the way it developed, so I scrapped it."

"A story about a guy who undergoes brain surgery. Hmm … sounds interesting to me."

"Well, maybe I'll go back to it, but not for a while. Right now I need to concentrate on my cooking and especially my dancing." He smiled. "Let's check out the video store."

Back in Julia's apartment they watched an old classic, *The Treasure of the Sierra Madre,* and followed it with a light lunch: leftover egg rolls and a box of fried rice that had way too much egg. Later, as it approached 3:00 p.m., Marco got up to leave.

Julia walked him to the door. "I've thought it over, and I think you should spend the night," she said unexpectedly.

Marco looked at her. "Are you sure?" He held back a smile. "I don't want you to think—"

"I'm sure." She nodded. "It doesn't have to be tonight. It can be tomorrow or the next day. I'll leave it up to you."

Marco hesitated. "Tomorrow is fine. I'll pack some things and come over after I get off work." He kissed her goodbye and hurried out the door.

36

Late evening

"WH-WHAT ARE YOU DOING HERE?" Marco said as he strode toward her. Angela sat on the steps that led to his apartment. He didn't know whether to hug her or wait for an explanation.

"We need to talk." Her tone matched her somber expression. "I'm worried about you, especially after our last conversation."

"You didn't have to come here. I'm doing fine, really I am."

"No, you're not," she shot back.

Finally, he reached over and gave her an awkward hug. "Let me help you with that." He picked up her luggage and led the way up the stairs and into his apartment. "You must be hungry. Can I fix you a sandwich or whatever you're hankering?"

"I had something in Dallas in between flights, but I would like a glass of wine. White if you have it."

He took a moment to pour some wine into two glasses and cut up slices of salami and provolone. He brought them over to the coffee table in front of the couch.

"I want to meet her." She picked up her glass and took a quick sip.

Startled, Marco didn't know what to say. He reached for his wine. "I don't think it would be a good idea. I mean, she's not well and not up to having visitors."

"Don't worry. I'm not going to tell her about your tumor. I just want to meet her. I want to see for myself … what she's like and why she has such a hold on you. Does she even know you have a sister?"

"Of course. The thing is, I was supposed to go over to her apartment tomorrow night and maybe spend …" He stopped himself. The less she knew about his plans, the better. "I'll talk to her in the morning and tell her you're in town. Maybe we'll drive over to her apartment. She tires easily and would only see us if she's having a good day."

Angela took another sip of her wine. "Tell her I'm looking forward to meeting her, if not tomorrow, maybe the day after."

Marco nodded. "She'll like you, I'm sure. She knows everything, by the way. About Susan, the accident, and the reason I came here to meet her. I put everything in a letter the day I set out to go back to Miami. After she read it, she called and said she wanted to see me. I have no regrets about coming back. I only wish I had told her all about Susan from the very beginning."

"Tell me the truth. Is there no hope for her?"

Marco sipped his wine and leaned back on the couch. "If you believe in miracles, she still has a chance. But the reality is she's getting weaker with each passing day. Her doctor has basically given up on her, which means the end may come at any moment." He swallowed hard and took a big gulp of wine. "She's counting on me to be there for her. She has no one else to help her."

"I'm glad we're having this conversation because … I know how this must sound, but when we talked on the phone, I thought only of you. I didn't want to hear about Julia or her problems. I'm sorry that your trip here didn't turn out the way you had imagined."

"But it did. After losing Susan, I never thought I'd find another soul mate. I consider myself fortunate in having found a new one in Julia. Most people go through their entire lives searching for that one person, that one soul who will complement them in every way. I was fortunate to have met two wonderful women. I'll die a happy man, knowing that fate brought me here to this place, at this time. I have no regrets."

Angela sipped her wine. "I really admire you, Marco. Any other man would've given up on her." She placed her hand over his. "There's something else we need to discuss. I know you don't want to hear it, but you have to make another appointment with the doctor."

"Look, Sis, I know it's important but I'd rather not talk about it." He got up, went to the kitchen and returned with the bottle of wine. "Like I said on the phone, I feel fine." He poured some more into each glass.

"What if something were to happen to you before … well, you know what I'm trying to say. Who would look after Julia?" She paused. "If she knew about your tumor, she would insist you have the operation. Am I right?"

Marco sighed. "She would be on my back about it, just as you're doing right now. That's one of the reasons I didn't tell her. Besides, I think her situation is much more critical than mine."

"How can you say that when you haven't seen a doctor since you left Miami? Things could be going on in your head that you're not aware of. You said yourself you had occasional headaches. Why take unnecessary chances?" She crossed her arms. "You're being very stubborn, so why don't we compromise?"

"What do you mean?"

"Well, if you promise to make another appointment, I'll pack up and go back to Miami."

"That's not a compromise."

"Oh, but it is, because I'm not leaving this apartment until you make a new appointment. I love you Marco, and I'll do whatever it takes to make sure you see a doctor. Either you make an appointment, or I'll stay here indefinitely. The choice is up to you." She relaxed her arms.

Marco thought about it for a moment. "Okay, Sis. You win. I'll call the doctor's office first thing in the morning. But I warn you, it's only for a consultation. I'm not having an operation until—"

"I know." She nodded. "We'll take it one step at a time." She took a sip of her wine. "Is your offer to fix something for me still open? I don't know why but I'm suddenly hungry. Maybe it's because we got this heavy stuff out of the way."

Marco smiled. "I know you like Mexican food, so let me make something that you've probably never had before. I got this recipe from one of the cooks at the restaurant where I work. It's an egg dish with fried tortilla strips and some salsa poured over it right before serving. It's called chilaquiles. You'll love it." He stood up. "You can have my bed, if you want. I'll sleep on the couch."

"That won't be necessary, but I would like to change into something more comfortable. By the way, I brought some old photos of us when we lived in Key Largo. Thought you might like to see them."

Minutes later, Angela sat down to eat. "It's delicious. You'll have to give me the recipe." They stayed up till midnight looking over the photos and reminiscing about their formative years in South Florida.

"Hadn't seen this one in ages." Marco held up a picture of himself dressed in a baggy little league uniform. "So many memories," he said wistfully. "You sure you don't want to sleep in my bedroom? I don't mind taking the couch."

"I've disrupted your night enough, don't you think?" She smiled. "See you in the morning."

Marco stayed up for a while longer. He hadn't planned to write in his journal, but Angela's unexpected visit prompted him to jot down some thoughts.

Angela was the last person I expected to see waiting for me on the steps to my apartment. I was happy to see her, but I worry that when she meets Julia, she'll say something about my tumor, though she promised she wouldn't. Tomorrow, when I call Julia, I'll tell her my sister arrived unexpectedly. Angela can be overbearing and I hope Julia won't be intimidated by her. Most of all I hope they hit off, but if they don't, there's nothing I can do about it.

Right now, I have mixed feelings about Angela and her reasons for being here. I know she means well, and I can't fault her for that. But she couldn't have picked a worse time. All day long, I had been thinking about Julia and how we were going to spend the night, the entire night together. The thought of it still brings a smile to my face. I love my sister, but I hope her visit is a short one.

Marco put down his pen. A second later, he picked it up again and wrote a brief postscript that summed up his feelings about Julia and her uncertain future.

Later, around two o'clock he awoke from a dream. Julia lay in a hospital bed with his sister Angela on one side and a ghostly image of Susan on the other. Across the room stood a priest and a nurse dressed in black. What did it mean? He shook his head and tried to go back to sleep.

37

"GOOD MORNING, SLEEPYHEAD," Angela said, the moment Marco emerged from the bedroom. "I got up early so I could beat you to the kitchen."

Marco held back a yawn. "Smells good, but you really didn't have to cook. I was going to take you out for breakfast."

"Well, I've got everything done, so sit down before it gets cold. Here, let me pour you some coffee." She picked up the French pot and filled his cup to the brim.

"Give me a second. I want to call Julia to let her know you're in town." He dialed her number and went back into the bedroom. Minutes later, he returned and sat down in front of a warmed-over bagel, Canadian bacon, and eggs over easy.

Angela sat across from him.

"When I told Julia that you wanted to meet her she kind of freaked out. She said the place was a mess and needed some time to do a little cleaning. I told her not to worry about it." He shrugged. "What can I say? She wants to make a good impression. I told her we'd be there between twelve-thirty and one." He took a sip of his coffee. "After I hung up, I called Dr. Molinar's office and made an appointment, just like I said I would. For next Thursday, a week from today."

A mild glow came over her face. "I'm so glad to hear that. Now, let's eat."

•   •   •

They were a few minutes early and sat in the car with the windows rolled down.

When Julia stepped onto the balcony, Marco saw her and waved. She waved back and motioned for them to come up.

Julia greeted them at the door. "I'm so glad to meet you." She reached to shake Angela's hand.

"Marco has told me a lot about you. All good by the way," Angela said, as though to make her feel at ease. She glanced around the room. "You have a beautiful apartment."

"I try to make it as comfortable as possible. Please have a seat. Can I offer you some wine?"

"I'll help you," Marco said, before Angela could answer. "Just sit down and relax. The two of you can talk and get to know each other."

A little while later, Angela asked, "Marco, can you give us a few minutes alone?" A mischievous smile crossed Angela's face. "I'd like to have a girl-to-girl chat with Julia."

Caught off guard, Marco hesitated. He looked at Julia. "I guess I can take a short walk or maybe go to the deli to pick up something for lunch." He stood up and made his way to the door. "Take your time." He had neared his car when he stopped and looked back. For a second, he worried that Angela might let something slip about his tumor. A familiar knot grew in the pit of his stomach. It lessened as he got in and drove away.

He returned a half hour later and gave himself a minute. Then he went back into the apartment. "So what did you two talk about?" he said with a nervous smile. He carried an antipasto platter and set it on the kitchen table.

Angela and Julia looked at each and laughed. "Just girl talk," Julia said.

"I wanted to get to know Julia without having to worry about what I could or couldn't say in front of you. Not that I planned to say anything bad or whatever. Anyway, we had a good talk and found we had a lot in common—besides you." Angela turned to Julia and smiled.

"Well, I'm glad you two hit it off. I brought something for lunch. Nothing fancy. Just something to tide us over until dinner."

Julia and Angela joined Marco at the kitchen table. They ate the antipasto and when they were finished, moved back to the couch. They continued to talk and sip their wine. Finally, Marco looked at Julia and put a protective arm around her. "We could talk for the rest of the afternoon, but I think Julia should rest or take a nap." He stood up.

"I *am* getting a little tired." She walked them to the door. Marco smiled to himself as they said their goodbyes.

The afternoon had gone better than expected, though he wondered what Julia and Angela had talked about.

Later, as they drove back to Marco's apartment, Angela said something that took him by surprise. "You know I don't believe in all that stuff about Susan's spirit being inside Julia, but … how can I say this? I noticed something about her. Something I can't quite describe—that reminded me of Susan. They don't look at all alike, so it wasn't her features, not even the way she spoke. It was more like a feeling, if it makes any sense."

"You mean … like a presence?"

"I guess so, if that's the right word."

They looked at each other but didn't say anything.

"So, what did you think of her?" Marco said, after a moment.

"I like her, and I can see why you two hit it off so well. She was very open with me, about her heart, about meeting you. About life in general. I wish we lived closer so I could be her friend or whatever. I gave her my phone number and told her to call me anytime."

Marco smiled. "I knew you'd like her. In a way I'm glad you came, so you could see for yourself why I'm so crazy about her. Thanks, Sis."

"For what?"

"For caring about me the way you do, and yes, for worrying about me the way Mom did."

Angela stifled a laugh. "That's what big sisters are for."

Back in Marco's apartment, she took off her shoes and sat on the couch. "Do you mind if I take a short nap? I didn't sleep well last night."

"Of course not. You can have my bed. I need to run an errand. Nap as long as you want. Maybe later we'll go to Fronimo's—that's where I work part time—and have coffee and some baklava."

"Before you go." She hesitated. "I thought I might leave tomorrow morning. I told my boss I had a family emergency to take care of, which is true. But now that I've met Julia and you've made a doctor's appointment, well, I've accomplished what I set out to do." She grinned and wagged a finger at him. "If I even suspect that you canceled, I'll be on the first flight to Tucson. Now go on and get out of here so I can take a nap."

Marco laughed. "I'll be back in a couple of hours."

38

IN THE MORNING, Angela took her time getting ready while Marco made breakfast. "Maybe we can stop by Julia's apartment on the way to the airport," she said from across the room. "I'd like to say goodbye."

"Good idea. If we have time, we might even drive through the city, so you can see some of the sights, like the pedestrian bridge made to look like a giant rattlesnake, and the aircraft boneyard where they keep the old planes from the past."

She smiled. "You know what I *really* want to do? I'd like to see the studio where you dance. I'm curious to know where it all began: the lessons, meeting Julia for the first time. It would be fun, don't you think?"

"Sure. If that's where you want to go, we can drop in after we visit Julia. I'll introduce you to Ramona. She took over as my teacher after Julia became too sick to work. She's a great teacher and a good friend of Julia's. In fact, she's the one who brought her out here."

After breakfast, Marco called Julia to let her know they'd be dropping by for a quick visit. "She's taking a late morning flight

165

back to Miami. We can't stay long. She wants to see the studio where I met you for the first time." He chuckled.

"Good. I have something to give her."

"What is it?"

"You'll see. Can you give me an extra ten minutes while I put my face on?"

"Take your time. It's early and Angela is still packing her bag." He paused. "About sleeping over, the way we planned …"

"I'm looking forward to it."

Marco smiled. "For a second, I thought you changed your mind. See you in a few minutes."

Julia greeted them at the door and led the way to the couch.

They talked for about fifteen minutes, then Julia pulled out a photo and handed it to Angela. "We were at a surprise party for me at the ballroom when someone took our picture. You can keep it. I have an extra copy. My friend Ramona dropped them off yesterday right after you and Marco had left."

Angela held it in her hand. "Thank you, Julia. I'll put it in a frame. I wish I could stay longer but Marco promised to take me to the studio where he learned to dance. Like I told him, I want to see where it all began."

Julia looked at Marco. "You'll have to dance with Ramona so she can see the progress you've made."

"We probably won't be there that long." He gave a small shrug. "We'll see." He looked at Angela and they stood up simultaneously.

Angela put her arms around Julia. "Remember what I said before. If you feel like talking … about anything, call me. I'll keep you in my prayers." She followed Marco out of the apartment.

When they arrived at the studio, Ramona took a moment to greet them. "Julia called a few minutes ago and said you were on your way." She reached to shake Angela's hand as Marco made a quick introduction.

Marco recognized a couple of students on the other side of the studio, and he waved to them. Another couple, whom he'd seen once or twice before took to the floor. Their bodies pressed tightly against each other, they danced a slow tango.

Angela kept her eyes on them as they came within a few feet and she turned to Marco. "Can you dance like that?"

"Well, I'm not as good as they are and it's definitely not my best dance."

"He dances the tango very well." Ramona smiled. "Let's show her." She grabbed Marco's hand and led him to the line of dance, near the corner of the room.

Marco got into the proper frame, then wrapped his arm around Ramona. He took a series of cat-like steps as he executed one pattern after another. When the music finally stopped, Marco relaxed his arms and ambled back to where Angela stood. She clapped loudly.

"I wish I'd brought a camera," Angela said. "I would've taken a couple of pictures. You were great, Marco. For a second you reminded me of Al Pacino in *Scent of a Woman.*"

"I owe it all to my two favorite teachers, Julia and Ramona. I'm living proof that even a guy with two left feet can learn how to dance."

Ramona laughed. "He's being modest. Julia would be the first to tell you he is a natural dancer. Did you show her the article that appeared in the paper?"

"What article?" Angela said with a puzzled look.

"Oh, it was nothing. Some reporter did a human interest story on me several weeks ago. She wanted to profile a single guy who's learning to dance. A photographer took a few pictures, which I don't think turned out that well. I meant to tell you about it but I guess I forgot."

"I have the article in my office," Ramona said. She disappeared into a back room and returned holding a copy. "You can keep it." She handed it to Angela.

Angela read the first couple of paragraphs. "They made you sound like a professional. And you're wrong about the pictures. They're great. Thank you, Ramona."

Marco glanced at the clock on the wall, which ran ten minutes behind to compensate for tardy students. "Well, I think we'd better get going. Don't want to miss the flight."

He and Angela exchanged hugs with Ramona, then left the studio. On the way to the airport, Marco's phone rang and he answered it on the first ring. "Sure," he said nodding. "But I have to leave early, no later than seven … seven thirty. See you later."

He hung up and turned to Angela. "That was Tracy from the restaurant. They're having a big party and she wanted me to help out for a few hours."

•　　•　　•

They strode into the terminal, checked in at the counter, then walked toward the security checkpoint. "I never thought I'd say this, but I worry about Julia," Angela said. "We exchanged phone numbers, so I hope she'll call me. But if she doesn't, I'm counting on you to keep me posted. I know you're in for some rough times and I want to be there … for both of you."

"Thanks, Sis. I knew I could count on you."

She sighed. "I wish my visit had been longer, but I left Miami in a bit of a hurry. I told my boss I wouldn't be gone for more than a couple of days. Maybe I'll call him in between flights—to let him know I'll be in tomorrow morning."

"I'm glad you came, Sis. Only next time I hope you'll call me so I know you're coming." He grinned, and after a moment became serious. "In a way I feel that what's happening in my life is a test. A test that I can't afford to fail. As you know, after Susan died I went into a deep funk and I don't want to go through that again. I know what you're thinking, but I'm much stronger now and I won't run away from it like I did before."

Angela nodded. "Good. I feel better hearing you say that." She hesitated. "I don't want you to think I'm being overly protective, but can you call me after you see the doctor?" She half-smiled. "And I don't mean a week later."

"I promise. I'll call you the moment I leave his office." He paused. "By the way … thanks for not telling Julia about my tumor."

As they neared the checkpoint, they took a moment to say goodbye. "Call me when you arrive in Miami," he said.

"I will." She gave him a hug and turned to join a line of passengers moving quickly through security.

Later, on the way to the restaurant, he dialed Julia. "Tracy called me a little while ago and asked if I could come in for a few hours. I probably should've said no."

"That's okay. I'm a bit tired and I need to take a nap. Just call before you leave the restaurant."

Marco smiled. "Maybe we'll stay up and have a glass of wine and listen to some music."

"I'd like that. Just try not to be too late."

"No problem. I told Tracy I had to leave before seventy-thirty. Talk to you later. Love you."

39

M ARCO SHOWED UP at Julia's apartment, carrying a small duffel bag and a couple of CDs.

"You were supposed to call me." She flashed a smile. "I don't have anything ready, not even an opened bottle of wine."

He dropped the duffel bag on the floor and gave her a quick kiss. "Don't worry. We have the whole night to uncork a bottle and do whatever we want."

"I've got a Merlot—from Argentina I think—that I bought at a wine tasting at CataVinos a few months ago. Shall we try it?"

"Sure. But first let me take a quick shower and get into something more comfortable. If you want, you can put on one of the CDs." He handed them to her. "They're two of my favorites. Norah Jones and Michael Bublé."

A moment later, Marco emerged from the bathroom wearing a pair of Dockers and a faded Miami Dolphins T-shirt. Julia had already opened the bottle and set it down on the coffee table along with some cheese and crackers. The Norah Jones CD played in the background.

He poured the wine. "To us, and the love that we share." He brought his glass up to hers. "May this be the first of many nights that we'll spend together."

They took a quick sip and after a moment, talked about Angela and her whirlwind visit.

"So, what did you and my sister talk about?"

Julia smiled. "Oh, just girl things … stuff that would bore you if you'd been a fly on the wall. She's very protective of you and asked a lot of questions, most of which I didn't mind answering except …" She took a sip of her wine.

"Except what?"

"Well, at one point when I told her how difficult it was for me to do things around the house, she asked if I'd thought about having you move in with me. I didn't expect her to say that, considering we had just met." She shook her head. "I'm not a good fibber, so I told her the truth. That we had talked about it but hadn't come to a decision."

"Good answer. Actually I'm glad she brought it up, because I've been thinking about it—a lot."

"Me too." She took a sip of wine. "Maybe after tonight you should bring the rest of your clothes and stuff."

"You really mean that? Not that I'm objecting. I'm just surprised you think it's a good idea."

Julia became quiet for a moment. "I've tried to convince myself that I can take care of myself, that I don't need anyone to look after me." She paused to steady her voice.

"But the truth is, I'm afraid, Marco. I can actually feel my heart getting weaker." She held his hand and snuggled up to him. "It took your sister's question to make me realize I can't do it alone." She sighed. "I'm sorry I didn't accept your offer to move in with me when you first brought it up. My pride and stubbornness got in the way of seeing things as they were rather than as I wished them to be."

He looked into her eyes. "It's okay. I'm here now and I'm not going to leave you." He kissed her as *The Nearness of You* played in the background. Then he stood and extended his hand. "It's our special song."

She got up slowly. "But we don't have a special song."

"We do now." He smiled.

She rested her head on his shoulder as they danced, barely moving their feet and staying in one spot throughout most of the song. When it ended, he kissed her and they held each other for several moments. His phone rang and he broke away to answer it.

"Hi Sis. Are you home already?"

"No, we're in the car, just leaving the airport." Brief pause. "On the plane, I had a lot of time to think about you and Julia. I really like her. Please let her know that I meant what I said about calling me. She's a special lady. I can see why you fell in love with her."

"I'll tell her you said that. I'm with her right now. We were dancing to one of my favorite songs. The night is still young and maybe we'll have one last dance before bedtime."

"She's dancing?" she said, a hint of concern in her voice.

"Don't worry, she's not overexerting herself. We mostly shuffled in one spot just like we used to do in high school." He chuckled.

"Well, give her my love and don't forget to—"

He nodded. "Yes, I know. I'll call you. Maybe everyday just to bug you." He hung up and joined Julia on the couch.

•　　•　　•

Angela turned to Mike. "I wish I had stayed longer."

"Why? Did something happen?"

She took a moment to answer. "I'm getting a bad feeling I can't quite describe. It got stronger as we landed in Miami." She shook her head. "It's mostly about Julia. When I first met her, I was taken aback. I didn't tell Marco this, but she looked very frail. Even her make-up couldn't cover up the dark circles around the eyes. I've seen it before when I volunteered at hospice. It's one of the signs that death is imminent."

"How long do they give her?"

"It's anybody's guess. Could be a few days, a few weeks …" She sighed. "I went there because I worried about Marco and now I'm just as concerned about Julia. If only they weren't so far away."

Mike slowed for a light. "So, what are you going to do?"

"I don't know. That's what makes it so frustrating. My biggest fear is that Julia will die suddenly and Marco won't be able to handle it. We talked about it and he said he wasn't going to go off the deep end like he did with Susan. Still, I worry about him. He's supposed to keep me posted." She lay her head back on the headrest. "I can't wait to get home and take a long, hot bath. I think better after I've soaked in the tub for at least twenty minutes."

Mike chuckled. "I kind of figured you'd say that so I got some take-out from La Carreta: *Ropa Vieja* with black beans and rice, and a double order of fried plantains. I'll heat it up while you're taking your bath."

Angela nodded. "Sounds good. If you don't mind, I need to close my eyes for a moment. Didn't get much sleep the past couple of days. Just nudge me when you pull into the driveway."

•   •   •

Back on the couch, Marco poured some more wine into their glasses. "As you heard, that was my sister, calling to say she had arrived safe and sound." He smiled. "She really liked you and she wanted me to let you know it. I'm glad you had some time alone to get to know each other, if only for a little while."

"You're lucky you have someone like Angela in your life. Someone who cares enough to come all this way just to see how you're doing. Too bad she couldn't have stayed longer. You could've taken her out to see the sights. If I were up to it the three of us could have gone out to lunch or maybe a picnic at Agua Caliente."

"Yeah, I wish she'd stayed a little longer. But she had to get back to work."

Julia sipped her wine. "When we talked, she said she was worried about you as though to explain why she had shown up without calling. She was kind of vague about it, which made me wonder why she even mentioned it." She half-frowned. "Is there something I should know?"

Marco picked up his glass and took a quick sip. "Not really. I have occasional headaches and I made the mistake of telling her about it.

She kept after me to see a doctor and I ignored her one too many times. Anyway, that's why she came here. To make sure I'd see a doctor. I made an appointment for next week." He sighed. "Sometimes she takes her big sister role more seriously than she should."

Julia smiled. "Nothing wrong with that. Makes me wish I had a big sister, just like Angela."

"I know you can't stay up too late, so I'll leave it up to you when you want to go to bed."

"I'm okay. Let's play another CD." She sipped her wine while Marco got up and put on another disk.

40

JULIA PUT HER HAND over her mouth to cover a yawn. "I hate to be a party pooper. Do you mind if we turn in?"

"No, not at all. You do look a bit tired."

They stood up. "Just give me a moment while I change and get myself ready for bed." She smiled. "It's a nightly ritual for us girls."

"Sure. I'll lock up and put everything away." He gave her a few extra minutes, then grabbed his bag and stepped into the bedroom. She'd turned off the lights and lay in bed facing a shuttered window.

For a second, Marco just stood there. Thoughts of Susan and the chain of events that had brought him to Tucson ran through his brain. Had fate played a trick on him? Everything happens for a reason, he had always heard.

He released a quiet sigh as he undressed and slipped into bed. "Goodnight, Julia. Sleep well."

"Goodnight," she said softy.

He heard her sobbing into the pillow. "What's the matter?"

She sniffled as she turned toward him. "I often cry myself to sleep. It's like my mind is releasing all the negative stuff that's going on around me." She blinked and caused the tears to trickle down her face. "I want you to know that I'm really glad you're here. I only wish I had asked you sooner."

He reached to brush her tears away. "It's okay. We're together and that's all that matters." He moved closer and pressed his lips to hers, gently at first, and then with a passion that he could no longer suppress. She only mildly resisted as he flung off the covers and began to caress her from the nape of her neck to the inside of her thighs.

Moments later, they looked at each other and smiled. "Are you okay?" he said, still breathing hard.

"I think so." She placed her hand over her heart and closed her eyes. "I just need to catch my breath."

He snuggled up to her. "I love you," he whispered. Then he kissed her on the forehead and stroked her hair with his hand.

"I love you, too." She fell asleep within seconds.

•   •   •

In the morning, slivers of light slipped through the cracks in the shutters. Julia opened her eyes and turned to Marco. "Wake up sleepy head." She nudged him gently. He looked like he was in a deep sleep.

"Marco, wake up. Wake up." No response. She shook him hard. Still no response. "Oh my, God. Something's wrong." She reached for his wrist and checked his pulse. Not good. She grabbed the phone on the nightstand and dialed for help.

When paramedics arrived, Marco lay unconscious. They checked his vital signs, then lifted him onto a gurney. Meanwhile, Julia dressed and gathered her things. She rode with him in the ambulance.

An hour later, an emergency physician emerged from the ER and spoke to Julia. "He's had a severe hemorrhage. The damage to his brain is extensive. It appears that he had a tumor which had been growing in his head for some time." The doctor spoke in a calm, detached manner.

Too numb to say anything coherent, Julia burst into tears.

"I'm sorry," he said, curtly.

"You're not giving up on him, are you?" Julia wiped the tears with her hand.

"Another neurosurgeon is with him right now. He'll give you a more complete explanation of his condition." He shook his head. "The prognosis is not good. In a case like this, all we can do is make him as comfortable as possible."

As comfortable as possible. Familiar words she'd heard just days before her mother died of cancer. She dreaded having to call Marco's sister. She took a moment to collect herself, then rummaged through her purse.

A long sigh, followed by a silent prayer as she dialed the number. She took a seat at the far end of the room, away from the noise of a television showing a baseball game in progress.

"May I speak to Angela? My name is Julia. We met when she was in town visiting Marco."

"You just missed her. She left to run a quick errand. Should be back in a few minutes. Can I take a message?"

Julia sniffled. "I'm afraid I have some bad news. Marco is in the hospital."

"What happened?"

"He had a brain hemorrhage. It doesn't look good. I'm here at the hospital, waiting for someone to give me more information. Please tell Angela to call me."

"Yes, of course." He sighed. "I don't know how I'm going to break it to her. She'll probably want to take the next plane to Tucson. Thank you for letting us know."

Julia sat back and closed her eyes for a moment. She was the sick one, not Marco. Nothing made sense. He came into her life and gave her a reason to want to live and fall in love again. But now it all seemed pointless. For a second she wished it had been her that paramedics rushed to the hospital. She covered her eyes as she wept quietly so as not to disturb the others: an elderly couple and a young pregnant woman with a little girl by her side.

Her phone rang and she took a deep breath before answering it.

"Tell me what happened," Angela said, her voice shaky. "Mike didn't give me any details."

"We spent the night together and when I woke up, I turned to Marco. I noticed something was wrong; he seemed unresponsive, so I called 911. When we got to the hospital, one of the doctors said he'd suffered a brain hemorrhage." She hesitated. "They're not holding out much hope for him."

Angela let out a wail that lasted several seconds. After a moment, she stopped crying. "It's my fault. I should have stayed with him and forced him to see the doctor while I was there. For weeks I had been telling him the tumor in his head was like a ticking bomb, but he ignored me. That's why I went there, to convince him that he had to see a doctor right away."

"He had a tumor? I-I don't know what to say. I had no idea that he had any medical problems. If he had only told me, I would have understood. We would've supported each other."

"He worried more about you than he did about himself. He even cancelled the surgery to remove the tumor. The odds were in his favor, but he didn't want to take a chance. He feared something would go wrong and he'd be unable to help you while you waited for a transplant. Believe me, I tried everything to get him to have the surgery." She sniffled. "I'm sorry but this is too much for me. I need to get off the phone. I'll call you when I arrive in Tucson."

Julia hung up and stared into space. Images of Marco filled her mind and she had to force herself to keep from crying. "God, please give me strength," she whispered.

41

"I just arrived," Angela said. "I want to see Marco, if only for a moment. Then I'll go to his apartment. Did they give you any more information?"

"A neurosurgeon came out to talk to me, but he didn't say much. He knew I wasn't a member of the family. I told him you'd be in town soon. He wants to meet with you around eight in the morning after he examines Marco. I'm home now but if you want, I can meet you at the hospital or go over to Marco's apartment."

Angela hesitated. "No. It's late and you really should get some rest. I'll just see you in the morning. Maybe we'll meet for coffee or something. There's a lot we have to talk about."

Julia nodded. "Okay, I'll see you in the morning." She hung up, then dialed Ramona's number. She'd meant to call her earlier but fell asleep on the couch. Her voice mail answered. She left a short message. "We need a miracle, Ramona. Please pray for him," she added.

Ramona called ten minutes later. "It doesn't make any sense. Marco seemed to be in perfect health. What happened?"

Julia held a glass of water in her hand and set it down. "He had a brain hemorrhage. He spent the night at my apartment. When I woke up, I tried shaking him, but he didn't respond. He appeared to be in a really deep sleep. That's when I called 911."

"He was here yesterday with his sister. He looked fine. We danced the tango to show her how well he could dance. I'm in shock. I don't understand how he could go from being healthy one day to lying in the hospital the next."

"When I talked to his sister, who's back in town, I found out that Marco had a brain tumor. He'd postponed an operation because he was afraid I'd be alone if something went wrong." She paused to wipe the tears from her face. "I don't know what to do. I go from crying all the time to wishing it was me lying in that hospital. One of the reasons I allowed myself to sleep with Marco was because I knew that time was running out for me. Little did I know it was running out for him as well."

"I know the next few days are going to be really hard for you." Her voice started to break. "Call me anytime, even if it's just to vent. I'll try to see Marco during one of my breaks. I'll say a prayer for him … and for you, too."

"Thanks, Ramona. I knew I could count on you."

Later as she sat on the couch, she thought about the instructions she'd left for Marco—her final wishes, to be read upon her death. She reached for *The Prophet* on the coffee table and removed the handwritten pages. She took a moment, then wrote a short addendum.

To whoever reads these words. Let it be known that my last and final wish is that I be buried next to Marco Anissi.

She placed the papers on the table, in plain view for anyone to see. Then she got up and poured herself a drink. Wine always made her sleepy and she prayed she'd fall asleep. She had survived the day, but with little hope that tomorrow would be any better.

•　　　•　　　•

Julia got to the hospital a little after 8:00 a.m. She saw Angela and a doctor whom she recognized as the neurosurgeon emerge from Marco's room. He shook her hand, then turned and walked away.

Julia approached Angela and gave her a big hug. "I want to see Marco. Give me a moment."

Angela nodded. "I'll wait for you downstairs in the coffee shop."

Julia stepped into the room and came around to the side of the bed. She leaned over and kissed him on the lips. "If you can hear me, please know that I love you. I love you very much." She picked up his hand and brought it up to her face, then set it back down.

She choked back her tears as she recited part of the 23rd Psalm she knew from memory. "The Lord is my Shepherd. I shall not want. He maketh me to lie down in green pastures. He leadeth me beside the still waters. He restoreth my soul. He leadeth me in the paths of righteousness. Yea, though I walk through the valley of the shadow of death, I will fear no evil. For thou art with me. Thy rod and thy staff, they comfort me."

A burly young man dressed in green scrubs entered the room. "I'm sorry but he's scheduled for an MRI. It shouldn't take long."

Julia stepped back while the young man pulled out the bed and rolled it through the doorway.

A moment later she joined Angela in the coffee shop. "How are you holding up?" She took a seat across from her.

"I should ask you the same question." She sighed. "You were carrying a heavy burden, even before Marco had the hemorrhage."

Julia pursed her lips and looked away for a second. "I'm a survivor. Ever since I had my transplant I've learned that I can't give in to fear or self-pity. I stumbled along the way, but I always bounced back. I had no choice. Then when Marco came into my life I felt more secure. I probably leaned on him more than I should have."

Angela pushed her coffee cup to the side. "I talked with the neurosurgeon. He was very blunt. There's nothing they can do for him. The damage is extensive. He thinks that Marco probably didn't feel anything when it happened. They'll keep him on oxygen until …" Her voice wobbled as she brushed back her tears. "Until I make the decision to remove it. He gave me no other options. I wish I knew what to do.”

Julia squeezed her hand. “I’m so sorry. Even though I knew his prognosis was poor, I still held out hope for the slightest miracle. Over the years, I’ve learned to prepare myself, physically and emotionally for all of life’s tribulations. Still, I don’t think I’m ready to accept that Marco might die before me. I love him as much as you do, so I want to say that no matter what you decide, I’ll support you.”

“Thank you for saying that.” Her lips quivered. “I barely know you but already I feel a bond between us—like sisters—that makes it easier for me to deal with everything that’s happened.”

They talked for a few minutes longer and later, at Julia’s suggestion, strolled over to the chapel on the other side of the hospital. A chaplain who wore a simple cross around his neck greeted them at the door. “I’ll sit and pray with you if you wish.”

Angela nodded. Later, when she mentioned Marco and the difficult burden that had been placed upon her, the man said, “God will give you the strength and wisdom to make the right decision. Do not rush it. Just be guided by a sign he will place before you.”

42

BACK IN MARCO'S APARTMENT, Angela dialed Mike's number. She got his voicemail and left a message. The clock on the nightstand said 9:28 p.m.

Mike called five minutes later. "I expected to hear from you earlier. What's going on? How's Marco?"

Angela sniffled, then burst into a crying jag that lasted several seconds. "He's not going to make it, Mike. There's nothing they can do for him. The only thing that's keeping him alive is a ventilator." She took a few breaths through her mouth. "They want me to decide whether to remove it."

"You mean …?"

She nodded "Yes. He'll die peacefully. At least that's what they told me."

"What about a second opinion?"

"That's already been done. The neurosurgeon I spoke with said it was standard procedure to bring in another specialist."

"Now I wish I had gone with you. Are you going to be okay? I can be there by tomorrow afternoon."

She let out a long sigh. "No, it's better you stay where you are, at least for now. Julia and I need this time together. I'm relying on her as much as she's relying on me. The poor thing was exhausted. She went home early to rest. I may call her, but I'm afraid to wake her if she's already in bed. I'm really worried about her. She looks like she could collapse at any moment. When I see her in the morning I may suggest she go back home and we'll get together later."

"How long are you going to give it? I mean …"

"I wish I knew. I met the hospital chaplain and he suggested I not rush my decision. I think he's right." She sat on Marco's bed and stared at a picture of Marco and Julia on the nightstand. "I stayed up late last night worrying and thinking about Marco. I hope I can get some sleep. I think I'll turn in early."

A half hour later, distorted images of Marco lying in bed hooked up to machines and monitors kept her awake. As much as she tried she couldn't sleep. She sat up, turned on the lamp, and looked for something to read. Something to clear her mind, for a moment at least. Through the partially opened drawer of the nightstand, she spotted a copy of *Gourmet*. She couldn't reach it and so stood up, then opened the drawer. A gray notebook partly obscured by the magazine caught her eye and she picked it up instead. Written across the top were the words *For the Love of Susan*. She hesitated a moment, then sat down and opened it.

She read one entry after another and paused to wipe the tears that blurred her vision. When she came to the last entry, written three days ago, she let out a moan.

If something were to happen to me, I want everyone to know that I wish to donate my heart to Julia Tinsley. I love her and want her to have a chance for a long, happy life.

His words comforted her in a way she hadn't expected. Was it the *sign* the chaplain said would appear before her? "Oh, Marco, even now you amaze me," she whispered.

She sobbed as she closed the notebook and turned off the lights.

43

THREE DAYS LATER, Julia lay in a hospital bed with Angela and Mike on one side and a young orderly on the other.

"I don't think I deserve it," Julia said, her eyes red from crying.

Angela squeezed her hand. "Of course you do. Marco's heart will soon be inside you, just like he wanted." She pursed her lips and nodded. "That makes you family. Later when you're up and around we can talk, and you can decide what you want to do. Of course, we'd love for you to come back to Florida. We have a big house with an extra bedroom. As a matter of fact, there's a dance studio less than a mile away." She caught an impatient look from the orderly. "Well, I think we should go. See you in a few hours." She leaned over and kissed her on the cheek.

Julia managed a weak smile. "Thank you. Thank you for everything."

Angela and Mike stepped into an adjoining room where Marco lay in a coma. A priest soon arrived and they gathered around the bed to say a prayer. "Hail Mary, full of grace, the Lord is with thee; blessed art thou among women, and blessed is the fruit of thy womb, Jesus. Holy Mary, Mother of God, pray for us sinners now and at the hour of our death."

They continued to pray as a technician disconnected the ventilator. Moments later, Marco stopped breathing. Mike and Angela hugged each other and stayed for a few minutes longer.

"Goodbye little brother," Angela said tearfully. She leaned over and kissed him on the forehead.

They left the room and meandered through connecting halls until they reached a large waiting area with a sign on the wall that said: FOR FAMILIES OF O.R. PATIENTS ONLY.

•   •   •

Five weeks later

Julia and Ramona sat at an outdoor table in front of a coffee shop on Fourth Avenue. "I love this place, this street," Julia said, smiling. "I wish Marco and I had come here. He would have enjoyed the funky shops and the offbeat characters that hang around the bars and restaurants." Her smile faded as she looked away for a moment.

"You okay?"

Julia nodded. "I'm doing better, but every now and then a rush of memories runs through my head and I have to take a deep breath to keep from crying." Her lips quivered. "It's not just the memories. Every night before going to bed, I touch my chest and I can feel Marco's heart beating inside me. You may think it's strange but sometimes I talk to him as though he were still alive. It's my way of coping with everything that's happened."

She hesitated. "There's something I want to share with you." She gave herself a moment, then continued.

"In the letter Marco wrote to me before leaving Tucson, he mentioned that his fiancée Susan had died in a car accident many years ago. He knew her heart had been donated to someone on a waiting list. Somehow he found out I had been the recipient. That's the reason he came here, to meet the girl with his fiancée's heart."

"You had his fiancée's heart?" Ramona's jaw dropped. "That's incredible. But I don't understand. Why did he want to meet you? Obviously it wasn't just to take dance lessons."

"This is where it gets really weird. Marco thought Susan had reached out to him and so he came here to find out—I know how this must sound—if we had a spiritual connection. I would have been skeptical if he'd told me earlier. But as I look back, there were too many things we had in common as though we'd known each other from a long time ago. I'm not into metaphysics or the occult, but I have to admit there was something … something indescribable that had brought us together. Ramona, he was the soul mate I had yearned for all my life." She sniffled as she ran her hand across her eyes.

"I don't know what to say." Ramona shook her head. "I'm stunned, absolutely stunned. Did his sister know about this? I mean about his wanting to meet the girl with Susan's heart?"

"Probably. Knowing her, I'm sure she tried to talk him out of it."

"Well, regardless of why or how it happened, I think you and Marco were a perfect match."

Julia smiled. "Yes, we were. Anyway, it was something I wanted to share with you because you're a good friend, and also because Marco thought so highly of you."

Ramona became quiet for a moment, then changed the subject. "Have you thought about what you're going to do? You know you're more than welcome to come back and teach at the studio." She smiled. "Everyone's been asking about you."

Julia sipped on her tea. "I appreciate the offer, but I think I want to hold off making definite plans at least until I get back from Miami. Marco's sister and her husband invited me to spend a few days with them and I said I would. It'll do me good to get away from here for a while. She and I talk every few days. She's been there for me since before and after the surgery." She paused. "They want me to move back there. Even offered to let me stay in their house until I get established."

"Is that something you'd want to do?"

Julia thought about it for a moment. "I'm not sure. Part of me would love to go back to Florida, but I think part of me would miss Tucson and its seductive lifestyle. I think what they say is true. You can't go home again. Especially when you've been away as long I have. I'm like a ship that's passed the halfway mark, the point of no return." She gave a quick chuckle.

"I almost forgot to tell you." Ramona took a sip of her tea. "My husband saw Max as he was pulling out of the parking lot at the gym where he used to work. You think he's back in town?"

"I don't know. Maybe." She gave a small shrug. "I thought about calling him, to let him know about Marco, but I was afraid he'd think I'm free to resume our relationship. Eventually I'll tell him. But not until I've had a chance to sort out my feelings about Marco, about myself and the idea that he and I will literally be bonded for the rest of my life." She sniffled, holding back her tears. "He gave me the gift of life, Ramona. It's like fate brought us together for reasons that neither one of us were meant to understand."

Ramona gave her a moment. "What do you say if we take a walk? Maybe check out a store or two. There's this neat little shop I discovered a couple of months ago. It has vintage clothing dating back to the twenties and thirties. I'd like to pick something up to incorporate in one of our dances. You can help me select an outfit, maybe even try it on."

She smiled. "That sounds like fun." She got up, ready to follow Ramona down the avenue. "If we have time, maybe we can go into one of the other shops. I need to buy a small gift for Angela."

44

A LETTER FOR MARCO with no return address arrived at Angela's house. *That's odd,* Angela thought. Marco never used her address. Curious, she tore it open and gasped as she read through it quickly. "Oh, my God! This can't be true." She shook her head and burst into tears.

"What is it?" Mike said.

"See for yourself." She handed him the letter.

Dear Marco,

I tried sending a letter to your old address, but it was returned. So, I decided to send it to your sister's home.

A few days ago, while talking to my husband about Susan, I let it slip that I had sent you information about the woman who had received Susan's heart. He didn't react until later when he said he needed to clear up a misunderstanding. He said that at the last moment, Susan's heart went to someone else, even though it was supposed to go to Julia Tinsley. My husband received the last minute notice but

191

didn't tell me, until now. He didn't want to upset me at the time. He kept the information regarding the recipient but misplaced it several years ago. I can try to look for it if you're still interested.

Sincerely,
Barbara Valencia.

"I'm … I'm speechless," Mike said. "It's like a bombshell from hell." He put the letter down on the coffee table. "Are you going to tell Julia?"

She crossed her arms and paced. "I don't know. Right now I'm angry and hurt. To think that what happened could have been avoided. It makes me want to scream." She stopped pacing. "Mrs. Valencia sure didn't do us any favors."

"Would it have been better if she'd kept the information to herself?"

She had to think about it. "In a way I wish she had." She stared at the picture of Marco and Julia that sat on the mantel. "It would have been easier for all of us."

Mike nodded but didn't say anything.

The phone rang and it startled them, slightly. "I'll get that." Mike stepped across the room. It was Julia, calling about her upcoming trip to Miami. He jotted down the flight and gate information.

"We'll be waiting for you," he said and hung up.

Moments later, Angela picked up the letter and took it to the kitchen.

"What are you doing?" Mike followed right behind her.

She dropped the paper in the sink and lit it with a spark from a match. "It's what Marco would have wanted. He was Julia's soul mate and I won't take that away from her … not now, not ever."

She turned on the water to wash away the ashes, and then calmly walked away.

ABOUT THE AUTHOR

Ernesto Patino is a multi-genre author whose books range from Mysteries and Thrillers to Romance and Children's books. His published works include *Enough to Make the Angels Weep, In the Shadow of a Stranger, Web of Secrets,* and *The Last of the Good Guys.* He lives in Southern Arizona with his wife Pamela with whom he shares a passion for ethnic cuisines, classical music and foreign films. He is a member of International Thriller Writers. For more information about Ernesto Patino, visit his website at *ernestopatino.com.*

YOU MIGHT ALSO ENJOY

MARGERY

Jeffrey Penn May

Introverted backpacker Jeremy wanders off trail and discovers an eccentric, otherworldly town nestled in a mountain basin.

MY ONLY FRIEND, THE END

Steven Owad

Surviving was easy. The hard part—living alone— starts now.

STILL LIFE

Paul Skenazy

When his wife, Edie, dies, Will Moran abandons all he used to be, and do, to paint still life canvases of rocks and driftwood on the walls of his house.

Available from Paper Angel Press in
hardcover, trade paperback, and digital editions
paperangelpress.com